Awards and Honors for

GIRL OF THE SOUTHERN SEA

- Finalist for the Governor General's Literary Award
- Honorable Mention for the NCTA Freeman Book Award
- Honor Book for the Malka Penn Award for Human Rights in Children's Literature
- Winner of the Northern Lights Book Award
- Finalist for the SYRCA Diamond Willow Award
- Finalist for the MYRCA Sundogs Award
- Finalist for the Red Cedar Fiction Award
- Finalist for the Hackmatack Children's Choice Book Award
- USBBY Outstanding International Book
- Rise: A Feminist Book Project List selection
- Bank Street Best Book
- Junior Library Guild selection
- *CCBC Best Books for Kids & Teens* ★ Starred Selection
- Forest of Reading Kid Committee Silver Birch Recommended Reading List selection

"In spare and elegant prose, Kadarusman weaves a quiet tale of survival, grit, and integrity....Peppered throughout are stories that Nia crafts, based on Indonesian legends about the princess of the Southern Sea. With nuanced characters, this is a lovely gem for fans of irrepressible girls and contemporary stories set outside of the U.S"*—Booklist*

Girl
of the
Southern
Sea

Michelle Kadarusman

pajamapress

Paperback edition first published in Canada and the United States in 2022
Hardcover edition first published in Canada and the United States in 2019

 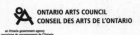

The publisher gratefully acknowledges the support of the Canada Council for the Arts and the Ontario Arts Council for its publishing program. We acknowledge the financial support of the Government of Canada through the Canada Book Fund (CBF) for our publishing activities.

Library and Archives Canada Cataloguing in Publication

Kadarusman, Michelle, 1969-, author
    Girl of the southern sea / Michelle Kadarusman.
ISBN 978-1-77278-081-9 (hardcover) | 978-1-77278-236-3 (softcover)
    I. Title.
PS8621.A33G57 2019   jC813'.6   C2018-905918-4

Publisher Cataloging-in-Publication Data (U.S.)

Names: Kadarusman, Michelle, 1969-, author.
Title: Girl of the Southern Sea / Michelle Kadarusman.
Description: Toronto, Ontario, Canada: Pajama Press, 2019. |Summary: "A 14-year-old girl living in the Jakarta slums who longs to be a writer sees an opportunity to raise money for school fees when she survives a minibus accident and the locals begin saying she has magical good luck. But when the crowd turns against her and she discovers her father's plan to marry her off to an older man, she must summon courage and conviction to write her own story."
— Provided by publisher.
Identifiers: ISBN 978-1-77278-081-9 (hardcover) | 978-1-77278-236-3 (softcover)
Subjects: LCSH: Poor children -- Indonesia – Juvenile fiction. | Authors – Juvenile fiction. | Teenage marriage – Juvenile fiction.| BISAC: JUVENILE FICTION / Social themes / Homelessness & Poverty. | JUVENILE FICTION / Social Themes / Self-Esteem & Self-Reliance.
Classification: LCC PZ7.K333Gi |DDC [F] – dc23

Cover Images—Fragoso Marin Fotografia, bayualam, Rosapompelmo/Shutterstock
Cover and book design—Rebecca Bender
Author photograph—Micah Ricardo Riedl

Manufactured by Friesens
Printed in Canada

Pajama Press Inc.
469 Richmond St. East, Toronto, Ontario, M5A 1R1

Distributed in Canada by UTP Distribution
5201 Dufferin Street Toronto, Ontario Canada, M3H 5T8

Distributed in the U.S. by Ingram Publisher Services
1 Ingram Blvd. La Vergne, TN 37086, USA

For girls all over the world,
fighting for the futures they deserve

Glossary

arak (ARR-ak) | An alcoholic spirit made from the fermentation and distillation of fruit or grain.

Bapak (ba-PA, the 'k' is usually silent) | Father or mister.

batik (BAH-tik) | A technique of wax-resist dyeing applied to cloth. The origins of the technique are from Java in Indonesia. Batik garments play a central role in ceremonies and traditional garments worn by both men and women.

Bubur (bu-BOOR) | An Indonesian congee, or rice porridge, usually made with white rice, chicken and flavored with spices. It is a common breakfast food.

Dangdut (dung-DUT) | A genre of music that is a mix of Indonesian folk, traditional, and popular music.

Dewi (DAY-we) | Princess or Goddess.

Ganja (GUN-ja) | The Indonesian and Hindi word for cannabis or marijuana. The term is also used in many countries around the world as a slang term for cannabis.

Hijab (HEE-jub) | A head covering worn in public by some Muslim women.

Ibu (ee-BOO) | Mother or Mrs.

Jaga (JUG-a) | (Also, penjaga): a caretaker.

kebaya (ke-BY-ya) | A Javanese traditional blouse/dress combination worn by women.

lumpia (LOOM-pia) | A fried spring roll commonly found in Indonesia. It is a savory snack made of a thin pastry wrapper with a filling, usually made up of noodles and vegetables.

martabak (mar-TA-buk) | A stuffed pancake (either sweet or savory) which is a common street food all over Indonesia.

Nyadran (NA-dren) | A traditional Javanese custom—placing flowers or food offerings on ancestral gravestones—practiced to welcome the fasting month of Ramadan. The origin of the tradition is traced back to Java's earlier Buddhist-Hindu culture.

Ramadan (rum-a-DAHN) | A holy month of fasting, observed by Muslims worldwide.

rupiah (roo-PEE-ah, both singular and plural) | the basic monetary unit of Indonesia.

sambal (sum-BAL) | A hot relish made with vegetables such as peppers and chillies or fruit and spices.

sarong (SAH-rong) | A traditional cloth worn by women and men throughout Southeast Asia. A sarong is made from batik cloth or printed cotton and shaped in a large rectangle. A sarong can be wrapped to create a variety of styles of dress. It has multiple other uses, from curtain to baby sling.

Indonesia

China

Japan

Pacific Ocean

Java

Bali

Indian Ocean

Australia

Java

Jakarta

Bogor

Lembang

Pelabuhan Ratu

1

Jakarta, Indonesia
The Chant

Three things a girl from the slum is told never to do.
Never go out after dark.
Never walk alone.
Never disobey your father.

Still, I am walking alone after midnight through a tangle of dark alleys. I have to find my *bapak* and bring him home. I move quickly and carefully through the inky darkness, willing myself into a thin shadow or a wisp of smoke. Lucky I am skinny and small. I wear a hoodie and hunch my shoulders like the boys do.

The slums are dark but not quiet. The humid night

air is filled with noise. I hear bottles smashing and men laughing. The sounds echo and distort as they bounce off tin walls.

It's surprising the ordinary things that run through a girl's mind when she is scared. Everyday things, like a fried banana recipe. *Flour, sugar, butter, egg...bananas! Flour, sugar, butter, egg...bananas!* I repeat the recipe in my head like a chant because it cheers me up and drowns out the sound of my heart pounding in my ears: *Flour, sugar, butter, egg...bananas!*

"Stay here," Bapak had said before he left. "Stay here and mind your brother. I will be home soon."

"Please don't go out tonight," I pleaded. "Don't leave us alone again." I gripped his arm. "I'm scared. What if those boys come to hurt us or steal from us?"

Bapak jerked his arm from my grasp. "Do as you're told," he said. "Go to sleep. Nothing will happen."

"But how do you know? What if the same thing happens that happened to Yuli's cousins?" Gang boys had broken into my friend Yuli's cousins' shack and stolen their cell phones.

"We don't have anything they want. Don't worry. I won't be long," he said. "Go to sleep."

"Please don't spend all the money," I said as he left, knowing it would make him angry.

He grunted and slammed the door. At least Bapak waited until Rudi was asleep before he left. At least Rudi could sleep peacefully thinking he was protected and safe.

I waited like Bapak told me. I lay next to Rudi on our shared mattress on the floor, listening to the howl and the rattle of the slum outside our tin walls. I lay listening, on alert for the marauding rodents that sometimes sneaked in and made off with our bananas. I lay listening, on guard for someone trying to open the door. And like many nights before, hour after hour, I lay listening for Bapak. But he did not return.

Rudi's breathing was heavy and deep. I eased myself up, careful not to disturb him. I crept outside, but just as I was relocking the door, I heard him call my name.

"Nia! Where are you?"

I ducked back inside. "Shhh!" I said, kneeling down on the mattress. "Stop screaming, I'm here."

Rudi threw his skinny arms around my waist. "But where were you? I was scared. Why aren't you sleeping? Where is Bapak?"

"I have to go and get him," I said, unfolding his arms from my body. "I won't be long, I promise. Go to sleep."

"No, Nia, no. Don't go. Don't leave me again." He launched himself at me, clinging tightly.

"I'm just going to Jango's hut," I said, keeping my voice calm. "It's not far. I will get Bapak and bring him right back. Remember what I told you about Bapak's broken heart? How he goes to Jango's hut to drink *arak* to help his heartache? I'm just going to tell him it's time to come home now. I will be back before you count to one hundred."

"But I don't know how to count to one hundred."

"Now is a good time to practice," I said. "Think of how impressed your teacher will be when you tell her you know how to count all the way to one hundred."

I left Rudi counting. I slipped out the door, careful to lock it behind me.

A hulking figure is looming toward me, swaying from side to side like an overloaded train carriage. He staggers closer and closer. Maybe my invisibility wish has come true, because he takes no notice of me at first. Then he stops. He laughs in a crazy way and lunges for me. I dodge his grasp, and he topples over in a heavy heap at my feet. His hands grope at my legs, but he stays on the ground. I kick him away and run on.

Go. Go. Go, I tell myself. *Keep moving*. I drop my head and run.

It is the gang boys I am most afraid of. Scrawny boys who huddle together, slapping each other around and babbling nonsense. Boys who band together in mean little crews. Boys who don't have enough *rupiah* to fill their bellies and are lightning fast. Just like the ones I can see up ahead blocking the alley. One is pounding on doors with a stick. I recognize one of the boys in the group. Arjun had been two years ahead of me at school. Back then, Arjun had worn his school uniform, shorts, and a button-up shirt. He had always helped the teacher clean the blackboard dusters. Now he wears a cutoff t-shirt to show his gang tattoo.

I stop in my tracks, hoping they haven't caught sight of me. I crouch in a doorway, my heart pounding. I can't let them see me, especially not Arjun. The gang is making its way toward me. The noise of the stick banging on doors is getting louder and louder. It is a matter of seconds before the stick finds the doorway I am crouching in. I throw myself into the garbage ditch that lies next to the dirt alleyway. I hold my breath and pray a rat won't run over me. I lie there frozen until they move past.

Once the laughter and the banging stick are far enough away, I crawl out of the ditch. Putrid garbage sticks to my hoodie and my legs. I wipe the grime off as well as I can and break into a run up the alley. I turn the corner and see Jango's arak hut where he brews up batches of the illegal alcohol. Jango sells any amount, from a splash in a plastic cup to bucketsful. He is not picky about his customers— anyone with rupiah is welcome to buy it.

A few men are squatting around a kerosene lamp, smoking clove cigarettes and playing dominos. Local *dangdut* music is blaring from an old radio perched on the shelf outside Jango's hut. People are staggering around attempting to dance. I look from face to face for Bapak.

It is his shirt I recognize first. He is wearing a green t-shirt with a logo of a German beer company on it. He is staggering around, but he is still standing.

"Bapak." I run to him and shake his arm. "Bapak, it's me. It's Nia. Come on, it's time to come home."

Bapak stares at me without seeing me. He looks confused. Then his focus shifts and he frowns. "Where is your brother?" he asks, swaying back and forth. "I told you to stay home."

"Rudi is still at home, Bapak. Come on, we have to get back to him."

"You left your brother alone," Bapak says, his words heavily slurred. He takes a step back. "You disobey your father." He trips, landing on his butt.

"Bapak," I say, bending down to him. "Come on. We need to get home. You must have some rest so you can work tomorrow, remember? You have to take the fried-banana cart to the train station early just like every day. Come on, Bapak. We have to get home to Rudi. Please."

"You left Rudi alone," he mumbles from the ground.

"Yes, Rudi is alone. Come on, get up. We have to go home so he won't be alone."

Jango comes over and kicks Bapak's feet. Jango is small and compact, always bouncing from one spot to another. He wears bright white trainers. "Go home, man," he says. "No more sauce for you tonight."

Bapak doesn't move. I try to pull him up, but he is dead weight.

"Will you help me get him home?" I ask Jango.

"Why would I do that?"

My only choice is to make a promise I cannot keep.

2

Chicken Bones

While Rudi and Bapak sleep, I go to the communal tap to fill our plastic water jugs with the water we need for cooking and cleaning. I put on a pot of water to boil to prepare the *bubur* for breakfast. I throw in the chicken bones from yesterday's scraps to help flavor the broth.

The morning air hangs heavy with heat. The rains have still not come, and even the early dawn doesn't provide relief from the suffocating temperature.

"Wake up, Rudi." I nudge Rudi once the bubur is ready. He is curled up on the mattress next to Bapak, who is snoring. A sour smell wafts from his body.

"Time for school, Rudi," I whisper.

Rudi opens one eye, like a tiger. "Big-boy school?" he asks.

"Yes," I say. "Big-boy school."

"Big-boy school with red shorts and my white shirt?"

"Yes."

Rudi buries his head under Bapak's sheet.

"I'm not ready for big-boy school today," he says from under the cover.

"Yes you are. Come on," I say, picking up one foot and tickling his toes.

Rudi wiggles farther under the blanket, kicking his feet furiously.

"I will stay a little boy today and be a big boy tomorrow," he says, giggling.

"Suit yourself," I say. "All the other boys will laugh and know you are not brave today."

Rudi's body stays motionless. His feet poke out from the blanket like small brown rabbit ears.

"Ah, well," I say, going back to the cooking area. "I suppose even little boys still need to eat their bubur. But only a small amount. Big boys would receive much more in their bowl." I let out a sigh and make a show of scooping the bubur loudly into bowls.

Rudi's face darts out from under the cover.

"Nia?"

"Hm?"

"I am a big boy today, I think."

"Really?" I ask. "That is a surprise to hear. Are you sure? I thought only a little boy lived here."

"No, really. I am big." Rudi scrambles out from under the blanket and stands up on his tiptoes. "See?"

"Ah, I see," I say, clapping my hands. "Come and eat your bubur then."

Rudi comes to the mat and sits down with me. He takes his bowl and we smile at each other. This has been our morning game since he started kindergarten.

"You lied, Nia," he says, spooning the warm rice porridge into his mouth. "You didn't come home after I counted to one hundred like you said you would."

"You said you couldn't count up to one hundred, silly."

I tip a splash of soy sauce in his bowl.

"Why can't you come to school with me?" Rudi asks.

"You know why," I say, "The government school is only free until the end of middle school. There are fees to attend high school, and we don't have the money."

Rudi nods. I don't know why he keeps asking, because he's heard me moan about it for months.

"Is Bapak going to have bubur with us?" he asks.

"No," I say, throwing a look at the sleeping shape under the cover. "He doesn't want his porridge this morning." I know enough that on the nights Bapak stays late at the arak hut, he doesn't have a stomach for breakfast the next day.

"Are you mad at Bapak?" Rudi asks.

"Stop asking so many questions," I say, getting up. "Besides, he is our bapak, and Mama taught me we have to respect our father no matter what."

"No matter what," says Rudi, with his hand on his hip as he mimics me.

"Stop being a monkey," I say. "Get dressed for school. I don't want to be late. *Ibu* Merah will be angry again."

I wait for Rudi to put on his school uniform and try hard to remember the good times with Bapak when I was little. When Mama was still alive and he did not drink. But things have not been good between Bapak and me for a long time now. He says he doesn't have the fees for high school. It's a lot of money for us, it's true. But he wastes rupiah on arak when he could be saving for my school fees instead.

"Hurry up. Brush your teeth and wash your face," I call to Rudi, putting his empty bowl in the big plastic bucket we use for washing dishes. "The boiled water is for your teeth."

Rudi returns to stand in front of me, still in his sleeping t-shirt, squirming and jumping up and down.

"Go to the pit latrine first then," I say.

"Come with me," says Rudi.

"You're brave, remember?" I say. "You can go to the pit by yourself now."

"No, please, Nia, please." Rudi hops from one foot to the other.

I put on my flip-flops. "Come on then," I say, motioning for him to put on his sandals. I take Rudi's hand and we walk through the narrow dirt alleys toward the pit latrine. I remember when I was a little girl I was afraid to go to the pit latrine alone too. Mama would tease me that no one had ever fallen into the pit, ever. But she would always go with me.

Sometimes the lineup is long, but not today. "Be careful where you step," I tell him.

I shift my weight from one foot to the other as I wait for Rudi. I have to go home and get Bapak up and moving, otherwise he won't find a good spot for the cart at the market outside the Pasar Senen Railway Station a short way up the train tracks from where we live. Senen station is the second largest train station after Gambir Station in central Jakarta.

When we arrive back home, Bapak is awake. His heavy shuffle and hooded eyelids betray his hangover. Rudi runs to him and throws his arms around Bapak's legs.

"You missed bubur," Rudi tells him.

Bapak doesn't return Rudi's hug. "I'll have something at the market," he says before prying Rudi off his legs. "Go to school."

Bapak takes the cup of tea that I hand him. He doesn't look me in the eye. His hand trembles as he lifts the cup to drink. I wonder if he remembers me finding him last night. If he does, he isn't saying so.

"The cart is ready, Bapak," I tell him. "I have mixed the

fritter batter to make the fried bananas."

Bapak nods again, finishes his tea, and slips on his sandals.

"I am ready too," announces Rudi, trying to get Bapak's attention. Rudi has managed to put on his school shorts, although his shirt is buttoned crooked.

Bapak wheels the fried-banana cart outside. His shoulders slouch as he pushes the cart along the bumpy dirt alley toward the train station.

"Goodbye, Bapak!" Rudi yells out the door. Bapak keeps walking, ignoring Rudi as usual. I try to hold Rudi's squirmy body still while I fix his buttons.

"Let's go," I say to Rudi.

We walk together to the local school, which I also attended until two months ago. The school is an old building with walls painted white and the roof painted blue like the sky. The chalkboards are cracked and the students squeeze together tightly in the small classrooms. The government school provides uniforms for the students, and volunteers cook a simple lunch of steamed rice and stewed beans every day for the children.

Rudi slips his hand from my grip as soon as he sees his best friend Jojo lined up along the wall of the school building. Yuli is my best friend, and Jojo is her younger brother—he is a year older than Rudi. The boys grew up like brothers because Yuli's mama took care of Rudi when he was a baby and I was at school. The two of them never stop fighting with each other, but they are inseparable. Rudi pushes his way roughly through the other children to stand next to Jojo.

I recross the road toward home, shielding my eyes from the swirling road dust. "See you after school," I call out, but my voice is lost in the noise of the traffic. I wave to the teacher, Ibu Merah, as she lines up the children along the low cement wall dividing the school building from the busy street. It is hard to say if she sees me with all the scooters, pedestrians, and rickshaws jostling for space. She turns her back and does not wave back.

I earned my middle-school certificate in November. High school has already started for those who can afford it. Now it is January. Without classes to attend, my days are long, boring, and filled with chores. Besides caring for Rudi and helping Bapak at the cart, I cook, do the laundry, and clean our home. All the duties that would have been Mama's if she were still alive.

When I get home, I wash up the dishes and scrub the dirty clothes in the big plastic bucket. Afterward, I hang the clothes to dry on a clothesline I string up inside our shack. I use the last of the morning's water to brush my teeth.

I look at my clothes folded in the corner and wish I could have a different dress to put on. Since I don't wear a school uniform anymore, it's harder to find nice clothes to wear every day.

I go to the mattress and sit down next to Mama's chest,

as I do every day. It is where her wedding *kebaya* are kept: a fine green lace blouse and a batik ceremonial *sarong*. I open the chest as I have done hundreds of times before. Slowly I take each item and spread it out on the mattress. I lift the garments and smell the fabric. Mama's scent is long gone, but I imagine I can still smell her. I hold the golden comb that she wore in her long thick hair on her wedding day. Mama's hair had been so dark and glossy that it had shone blue in the sunlight.

For a few moments I allow my mind to wander high above the tin rooftops, high above the shacks along the train tracks. My mind floats up and out of the slums, away from the garbage and the polluted river to a better place, where I am cradled in her arms again.

My daydream is broken by loud knocking on the door. My heart jumps. I catch my breath. It might be Jango!

Last night I had promised him something I could not possibly give.

3

Good Girls

I hold my breath, hoping Jango will go away.

"Nia! Open up. It's me." It's only Yuli.

I get up and open the door.

"What's wrong with you? You look as white as a ghost," says Yuli. She holds two empty water jugs. I motion for her to come inside.

"I thought it was Jango." I exhale.

"Jango? Why?"

"Because I promised him last night that I would give him double the rupiah that Bapak owes him."

"Why would you do a crazy thing like that?" She asks

as her pretty, dark eyes widen.

"Because I needed his help to get Bapak home, and money is the only thing he can't resist."

Yuli nods. She understands. "But how will you give him the money?"

"I haven't figured that out yet."

"Be careful, Nia. My mama always says that Jango remembers his debts."

"I'll think of something."

"I'm just on my way to get water. Come to my place after, okay?"

"Okay."

Yuli squeezes my hand before she leaves, heading toward the communal tap with her water jugs.

I steal an hour to spend with Yuli on most days after morning chores and before I go to the market to help Bapak at the cart. Yuli doesn't have the fees for high school either. It was my idea that we review our textbooks together every day to keep up our study practice, but Yuli's interest easily wanders. She prefers to flip through fashion magazines or read copies of the *Flying Gazette*, the local newspaper that commuters leave behind at the train station. Yuli doesn't share the same burning desire to go to high school that I do.

I sweep the wooden floor before setting out for Yuli's place. She lives along the train tracks like we do, farther up the rails toward the station and the market. On the way, I walk past Ibu Wangi's shop, where I buy the ingredients to make the fried bananas.

"Hello, girl," says Ibu Wangi, clapping her hands and making the fat on her arms jiggle. "You need kerosene for your cart today? My stock is running low, eh. If you need it, you should be a clever girl and plan ahead." Ibu Wangi taps her forehead meaningfully.

Ibu Wangi leans out of her open shop window, where she conducts her business. The window is at street level, so it's the perfect spot for her to survey the neighborhood.

"Hello, Ibu Wangi," I say. "I will let my bapak know."

Ibu Wangi studies me with eagle eyes. She stares me up and down, no doubt assessing if I am still a "good girl." She's let it be known that she can tell at a mere glance as soon as a young girl falls from grace. "People talk," she's said. "Not me, you understand. But other people around here are terrible gossips."

Ibu Wangi points her chin toward me, fanning her face with a copy of the *Flying Gazette*.

"Such a sad shame about your mama," she says, as she has said hundreds of times before. "Beautiful woman, your mama. So sad, so sad."

I nod.

"Shame, shame," she says, tut-tutting and shaking her head. "How old is your brother now?"

"He is five," I tell her, as she already well knows. Ibu Wangi feels the need to remind me at every meeting that my mama died giving birth to Rudi. "He has started school."

"Ah, time goes so fast," says Ibu Wangi. "And you, girl, how old are you?"

"I'm fourteen. I have graduated middle school," I say, looking impatiently in the other direction.

"What? And not started high school yet?"

I shake my head.

"Your mama used to tell everyone you would be a big-shot writer one day. You need to go to school to become a writer, you know."

"Yes, Ibu." I bow my head in respect, but I am thinking, *Mind your own business*. She knows very well that I can't go to high school because I don't have the fees.

Ibu Wangi flaps her copy of the *Flying Gazette* at me. "Maybe you will write stories for a newspaper like this one day, eh?" She snickers in a way that stirs a fire inside my belly.

Another customer comes by, saving me from more of Ibu Wangi's interrogation.

When I arrive at Yuli's house, I do my best Ibu Wangi impression, shaking my fists in the air and wiggling my bottom. "I can smell which girls are pure, good girls!" I mimic Ibu Wangi's squeaky voice, sniffing the air. "Come here, girl!" I say, lunging toward my friend. "Let me sniff you!"

Yuli rolls around on the mat, laughing and slapping me away.

"She is such a busybody," I say, sitting on the mat. "In my whole lifetime her shop has never run out of kerosene, but every week she tells me her stocks are low."

Yuli unfolds a copy of the *Flying Gazette*. "This will cheer you up. Listen to this." She scans the pages. "Here!" Yuli settles herself comfortably and grins as she reads the headline. *"Man from Bogor Turns Head 360 degrees!"* Yuli slaps her thigh and shrieks with laughter. "Can you imagine? Wow, I would totally freak out if I saw that."

"It's not true, silly. That paper is full of superstition and supernatural mumbo jumbo. Mr. Surat always told us we should not believe those stories."

Yuli makes a mock sad face when I mention our old school principal. "Are you putting down the *Flying Gazette*, my favorite newspaper? Besides, you write stories all the time."

"That's different. I don't pretend they are real."

She shakes the newspaper, her eyes shining. "But wait, you'll love this one...*Woman from Achang Eats Glass And Gives Birth to Porcelain Baby.*"

"Stop filling your head with nonsense. It's for people who don't know any better. Not for girls like us who are going to high school."

High school. If I keep saying it, it just might come true.

4

The Call

"We didn't always live along the train tracks," I tell Rudi that night. He couldn't sleep and Bapak was out again. "Our parents came from Lembang near Bandung in West Java. It takes five hours on a bus to get to Lembang. The ticket sellers say three hours, but the trip is always longer. When Bapak's father died, his land was divided into parcels. Bapak received the smallest one because he is the youngest. The land didn't have anything on it, just grass and goats. So he and Mama made a plan to come to the city to make money and return to the village once they had earned enough to build a house."

"What kind of house?" Rudi always asks.

"A nice house. Not like the one we live in now. Not shacks along the train tracks that shake like there's an earthquake every time a train goes by. Not shacks made of tin that are so badly patched together that waterfalls splash through the cracks when the big rains come. No. A good house with proper walls made of brick, with bedrooms upstairs and windows looking onto peaceful gardens."

"And the river," Rudi prods. "Mama's river."

"Mama used to say that there will be a clean river where we can drink the water and swim. The air around the river smells of frangipani and jasmine. We can eat bananas and mangoes from the trees, and there is plenty of shade and soft breezes to cool us from the heat. We will live a happy, peaceful life there."

Rudi squirms around, still restless. "Tell me about the gold letters on the cart," he says.

I rub my eyes. "When I was born, our parents had saved enough money to buy a food cart. It has wheels so you can push it around town and set up where you will get the best business. It has a space for a kerosene stove so you can cook and sell whatever you please. But first they had to think of what they would sell. And after that, they had to decide what the call would be."

"The call?" asks Rudi on cue.

"Yes, the call. All the food carts have a call. The noodle-soup cart has a *ting ting* bell, the chicken-satay cart has a *clop clop* bamboo drum, and the shrimp-cracker seller calls out *keeeeee*."

I yawn and Rudi pokes me with his sharp little elbow. "Stop it. I won't tell the story if you're going to be a monkey," I tell him. Rudi glues his arms against his sides.

"Bapak wanted to sell grilled corn but Mama wanted to cook fried bananas," I went on. "Her mama, she said, had taught her how to make the most delicious fried bananas, sprinkled with powdered sugar. Eating one of her banana fritters was like biting into a sweet cloud."

"And the call?"

"Everyone knows the fried-banana call is a cowbell."

"And did Bapak have a cowbell, Nia?"

"Yes he did. But it was my smile that decided it for them. Our parents said that after I was born and they saw me smile for the first time, they thought it was sweetest thing they had ever seen. They decided that my smile was a sign from God blessing us with good fortune, happiness, and prosperity. The cart would sell Nia's fried bananas and that's what they painted on the front in gold letters— NIA'S FRIED BANANAS—so it makes me famous too."

We both giggle in the darkness.

"Tell me the rest," says Rudi.

"It's late. Go to sleep now."

"Tell me about me being in Mama's belly."

"Not tonight."

"*Pleeese*, Nia?"

I sigh. He never grows tired of hearing the story, but I am weary from telling it.

"When I was nine years old, Mama told me that she had a baby in her belly. That was you. She was so happy to know you were coming. Late at night she let me feel you kicking around in there."

"Was I a good kicker, Nia?"

"Yes. She said you kicked like an angry water buffalo."

"Did she talk to me?"

"She used to sing to you and tell you how much she loved you."

"But she couldn't stay to meet me, could she?"

I swallow. "No. Mama had to make room for you in the world. So she left just as you were born."

"Where did she go?"

"She went to Heaven."

"Tell me about the piles of barbecued goat."

"Go to sleep. I'm tired now."

Rudi kicks his legs up and down on the mattress. "Finish the story," he whines.

"Stop it. I'll finish, but then you go right to sleep."

Rudi settles himself and waits for the story to resume.

"Bapak gave Mama the most beautiful burial anyone had ever seen." I blink and steady my breath. "He spent all of our savings on the funeral. We had an all-day feast with mounds of golden rice and piles of barbecued goat. Bapak honored Mama well." I lean my head against his. "After she was buried in the earth, I lay on top of the dirt to keep her warm."

Rudi reaches up and wipes away my tears with his little fingertips.

"That's enough for tonight," I whisper.

Rudi nods and holds my hand as we fall asleep.

5

Queen of the Southern Sea

Before she was known as Queen of the Southern Sea, she was known as the Princess of the Sun because she was so beautiful...

That's how Mama always began my favorite story. After the dinner plates had been cleared and the leftover rice and *sambal* put away for breakfast, Mama would sit on the mat in our shack with her legs crossed. "Come, baby." She would beckon me to her. Mama would wait to start the story once I had finally settled in her lap.

And so she would begin...

Princess Dewi Kadita was known as the Princess of the Sun because to gaze upon her face was like gazing upon divine light itself. The kingdom had never seen beauty like hers before.

King Munding was proud of his daughter, for not only was she beautiful, she was also kind and thoughtful. But he still grieved because he did not have a son to replace him as king.

King Munding decided to take a new wife who would give him a son, and so he married Queen Pearl, who before long produced a male heir. But seeing the king's continued devotion to his daughter, Queen Pearl began to worry that the princess would threaten her baby son's right to the throne. Queen Pearl demanded that the king banish Dewi Kadita from the palace. The king refused, saying that anyone who dared to speak ill of his daughter would themselves be thrown out of the palace. Queen Pearl quickly soothed the king by saying that she was mistaken. She acted so sweet and kind for so many days that he forgot she had ever suggested harm to his daughter.

But Queen Pearl had a plan. If the king would not banish the princess, the queen would find her own way.

One day before sunrise, Queen Pearl sent her maid to fetch a powerful witch from a nearby village. When the witch arrived, the queen took the old woman to Dewi Kadita's bedroom. And as she slept, the witch cast an evil curse upon the princess.

On that very day, the princess woke to find her entire body covered in awful blisters and boils. Her once smooth-as-silk skin was covered from head to toe with itchy scabs and ulcers that oozed puss and blood. Horrified, the princess ran to her father to show him her condition. The king ordered every healer in the kingdom to come to the palace to cure his daughter, but each and every healer failed. Queen Pearl whispered in her husband's ear that the disease was incurable and that it would be dangerous for Dewi Kadita to remain in the palace in case she infected their son. The king, unable to look upon his daughter's disfigurement any longer and fearing for his son's well-being, cast Dewi Kadita from the palace.

Poor Dewi Kadita covered herself in scarves to hide her disease. She could ask no one for help, as those who looked upon her were revolted at the sight of her affliction. Dewi wandered hopelessly and without purpose for seven days and seven nights. She slept alone in rice fields and ate the scraps that farmers threw to their ducks. Dewi slowly made her way to the edge of the Southern Sea. She had been to the seaside many times as a young princess and had happy memories there. She sat at the water's edge in the moonlight with tears streaming down her once-beautiful face. Something within her compelled her to enter the green waves of the ocean. A magical voice coming from the deep also encouraged her to plunge into the waters. To Dewi's astonishment, when she surfaced from the waves her skin was totally free of the sores and boils. In the water she was as pure and as beautiful as she had once been on the land. But as soon as she set foot on the sand her skin disease returned. Dewi Kadita would need to live forever in the sea, for not only did the salty waters cure her disease, but it also granted her eternal life.

And so the Queen of the Southern Sea, as she is now called, rules her watery kingdom with all the power of the Southern Ocean. But she is forever banished to the depths below the green waves.

I would always clap at the end of the story, and Mama would squeeze me and kiss my cheek. But when I was a little older I asked her, "Why does Dewi Kadita have to stay all alone in the sea? Why doesn't she leave the ocean and fight for her freedom on the land?"

Mama sighed. "It is an old, old Javanese folktale. I suppose it was told this way because people expect that a girl would choose her beauty over anything else. But maybe one day you will write your own version of the story about a girl who overcomes her hardships instead."

"I will, Mama," I told her. "I promise. I will write my own story."

Ever since then, I have written many adventures of Dewi Kadita: some of her conjuring tidal waves to conquer her evil step mother, others of her traipsing the world to find a cure for her curse. Some of Dewi's adventures are less serious, like the ones about her long seaweed hair or tricking sea serpents. But in all of my stories, Dewi Kadita finds a way to come out on top.

6

Offerings

$\mathcal{I}$ pick up Rudi from school the next day and we walk along the Ciliwung River toward the soccer field. We hold our noses from the stench rising from the polluted water. Ignoring their parents' warnings, children swim and play in the filthy river, looking for relief from the relentless sticky heat.

Rudi stops along the way to point and laugh at the kids jumping and splashing in the water. Lack of rain has left the river only knee deep.

"Why can't I go in too?" he asks.

"You know why," I say, pulling him along. "It's filled

with waste and garbage. You'd get sick from it. Besides, why would you want to? It stinks."

"It looks fun," he says, finally allowing me to drag him away.

"No." I push him ahead of me toward the soccer field. "You can have fun at the field instead."

We continue along the riverbank and skirt the old cemetery, where a small collection of ancient gravestones jut out from the ground. The graves are so old that the identity of those who lie there is long unknown. The names and dates are worn away, so those who live near-by take the reponsibility to ensure the cemetery is tended and the dead are honored.

I do my best to avoid the glaring reproach from the old woman, Ibu Jaga, whose unofficial duty it is to take care of the small cemetery plot. She sweeps the graves and keeps the area free of garbage and fallen leaves. To thank her for her efforts, the local folks leave a coin or two. Some say she has a third eye and can "see" things in the past and the future. Some say she can speak with the dead—as if her scarred face and hunched frame are not scary enough.

Mama used to prepare ceremonial flowers during *Nyadran*, the Javanese tradition of grave offerings before the holy month of *Ramadan*. She would buy the flowers at the market and pluck the petals, placing them in a small basket. "It is important to honor the dead, to honor our ancestors," she would say. "While we are alive, we should do good deeds for the ancestors so they will help us earn a good place in the afterlife. They will tell God we deserve a place in Heaven. Rose petals for love, jasmine for purity, pandan leaves for sweetness, ylang-ylang flowers for happiness, and frangipani for the eternal soul."

Sometimes Mama would place a frangipani flower behind my ear before we walked together to add our offerings to the collection at the cemetery gate. Ibu Jaga was always there to acknowledge our contribution with a small nod. Ibu Jaga knew who made the most thoughtful and intricate offerings. She knew who among us were the most devout, and she knew those who had allowed themselves to lapse.

I had not bothered with Nyadran offerings in the years since Mama died. I keep my head turned as we walk by Ibu Jaga, who sits like a statue under the shade of the acacia tree next to the cemetery. I can feel her judgmental stare drilling into me, and I shudder.

"Catch me, Nia!" Rudi runs ahead toward the soccer field.

"Go! Go!" I motion to him. "I will catch up."

This afternoon, like most afternoons, I take Rudi to the soccer field next to the train tracks. It's not really a field at all, but a large square of compacted dirt smoothed down by hundreds of bare feet. Boys kick balls around, showing off for the girls. The girls pretend not to notice, and gather in groups to talk over the important news of the day.

The younger kids play tag while they watch for oncoming trains. Some of the kids run alongside the slow-moving carriages as they rattle past. Sometimes the trains are so full that commuters cling to the side of the train or sit on top of the carriages. The little kids jump and wave to the commuters.

A girl from my old class—we all called her Big Sula because she is so tall—finds me in the crowd when I arrive at the soccer field. We haven't seen each other since our graduation. She wraps her large, sweaty hand around mine and pulls me toward her.

"High school is wonderful, Nia," she rasps in my ear. "We have beautiful uniforms and thick textbooks." She grins. "And the teachers are so intelligent! They are teaching us many subjects. Subjects that will make us smart just like them." Big Sula makes a clucking sound as she towers over me. "Too bad your bapak drinks away your high-school fees. Just as well you know how to cook fritters. I guess you will never be a writer like you always bragged about."

I pull my hand away and give her my best evil eye but she just laughs and walks away. Yuli comes by me and flaps her hand at Big Sula as she pushes her way through the crowd.

"Ignore her," says Yuli. "She's just jealous of you, Nia."

I shake my head at how stupid that is. "Her mama owns the Glorious Swan Beauty Salon, so Big Sula has enough money to go to school and do what she wants. Why would she be jealous of me?"

"Because you always got better grades. She knows that she will never be as smart as you."

"Huh. You'd think a girl who doesn't have to worry about school fees and who always has a belly full of warm rice would be nice at least."

Yuli's brother Jojo comes crashing through the crowd toward us. He still has his tray of batteries, peanuts, and candy strapped around his neck from hawking them along the street.

"Nia! Nia!" he shouts. "Your bapak! It's your bapak!" He stops to catch his breath. "At the market," he says, waving in the direction of the train station. "The police have hurt him! The police have taken your bapak away!"

"What is this?" I say, grabbing Jojo by his shoulders. "Is this a joke?"

"No, I am telling you the truth," he says, still panting. "They beat him. They beat your bapak."

I push Rudi toward the older boy. "Stay with Jojo," I order Rudi, before taking off toward the train station as fast as I can run. Yuli follows on my heels.

We arrive at the food stalls outside the station in record speed. I expect to see all kinds of mayhem, but the bustling market looks like any other day. Crowds of commuters rush and push, and hawkers shout and sell their goods. The air is thick with smoke from the satay sellers.

All is normal, except that Bapak is not at the fried-banana cart, which stands abandoned.

Bapak is nowhere to be seen.

7

Tutti Frutti

We rush to the empty banana cart.

"What happened?" I gasp, practically throwing myself on Mama Tutti. I put my hand on my heart to try to steady my breathing. Yuli clings to my arm.

Mama Tutti owns a fruit stall called Tutti Frutti, so everyone calls her Mama Tutti. Bapak had set up the fried-banana cart next to the Tutti Frutti stand as usual.

"It was bad," she says, shaking her head. "Bad." Only one of Mama Tutti's eyes meets mine because her other one is "lazy" and goes cockeyed when she gets upset. "Two policemen came sniffing around. The same officers from

Senen Jaya Metro, who always bother us for bribe money."

I nod, eager for her to continue.

Mama Tutti snorts. "And what do we get for the money we pay them? Nothing is what! It is harassment! Just to show us who is boss. Because they can, that's all." She flaps her arms around before sitting on a stool in the shade of her umbrella. "I can usually get out of it by giving them a bag of mangoes." She points to her fruit table, her lazy eye still jiggling. "But your father, he was in rough shape. Usually he plays along and gives them something. Today he had nothing. No rupiah. And what's worse, he challenged them." She slaps her thighs. "He told them to go and fleece someone else. One of the policemen pulled out his gun and started waving it around." Mama Tutti exhales in one long breath. "Then your bapak, he knew he was in trouble. He offered to make them some fresh fritters, but it was too late. The police were mad."

Mama Tutti hesitates and fans herself with a newspaper. She seems to ponder whether or not she should continue. Both eyes have finally settled in the same direction.

"Tell me," I say.

"They started to beat your bapak," she says, quietly now. "They pushed him down and kicked him, saying they would take his drunken behind to jail and confiscate the cart."

I cover my face, not wanting to hear. Yuli puts her arm around my shoulders.

"In the struggle, one of the police must have tipped

the fry pan. The hot oil from the pan splashed up on your bapak. He was howling in pain like a speared boar." Mama Tutti clasps her hands together on her chest. "But at least it stopped them from beating him anymore."

"And then what happened?" I urge her.

"They dragged him away. He was still screaming."

I slump into Yuli. My head is spinning.

"What do I do?"

"At least they didn't take the cart. You should get it away from here," says Mama Tutti. "Get it away before they come back and confiscate it like they said they would."

Mama Tutti is right. I go to the cart and look it over. The fry pan is upturned on the ground. Hot oil is seeping into the earth. I check the compartment behind the kerosene bottle where Bapak keeps the box for rupiah. It's empty.

I look over at Mama Tutti in her parrot-print sarong, gray hair peeking out from underneath her matching headscarf. She swats flies away from her fruit with deep concentration. I have known her since I was a child. She is family, of sorts. I know she would not lie to me.

"There's nothing there. He gave it all to Jango before the police came," Mama Tutti says before a customer diverts her attention.

I turn to Yuli. "Jango must have come to Bapak and asked for the double rupiah I promised him."

"But the police?"

"Bapak must have given Jango all his money, so he didn't have bribe money for the police."

Yuli nods. "I don't envy you, Nia. He will be as mad as a snake."

"I know. Mad enough to give the police his tongue and get himself beaten up."

Yuli helps me pick up the cowbell, fry pan, and utensils that are scattered on the ground. We put them back in the cart. I pack away the remaining batter and make sure the kerosene stove is turned off.

"Did you hear a dog howl last night?" Mama Tutti asks me once she has finished with her customer. She stands with one hand on her bony hip. "It means bad luck to hear a dog howl at night, you know." Mama Tutti is always telling people her old-timey superstitions.

"There are street dogs all over the city," I say. "They're always barking."

"Not barking. Howling. Think," says Mama Tutti, tapping her head. "Barking and howling are totally different."

"I don't remember," I say.

Mama Tutti frowns as if the whole thing were my fault somehow because I can't remember if I'd heard a dog howl.

I turn to Yuli. "Please help me push the cart home," I say. "Then I need to go to the police station and get Bapak out."

Yuli nods. "Let's go," she says.

"Here," says Mama Tutti, handing us each a star fruit. "Sorry for your trouble, girl." She pats my shoulder. "Take care now." I put the star fruit in my pocket. It will be a treat to eat with Rudi later.

We thank Mama Tutti and set off, pushing the cart through the thick crowd toward home. It is hard going. The cart is heavy and the path is bumpy and rough. The wheels on the cart are rickety and don't steer easily. The road is marked with deep potholes and busy with people, motorbikes, and minibuses. We stop a few times along the way to catch our breath and rest our arms.

"Come on," I say to Yuli. "Not too far now."

"You owe me some banana fritters for this," says Yuli, bumping my shoulder with hers. I know she is trying to cheer me up, but I can't bring myself to joke along.

We finally arrive home and set the cart down. I run inside to the secret hiding spot in the old teakettle, where the money is kept. I will need money to get Bapak out of the police station, and if he is hurt like Mama Tutti says he is, for the hospital as well. A small roll of bills is inside the cloth. I take all of it, burying the wad deep in my hoodie pocket.

"I'm going to the Senen Jaya Metro," I tell Yuli. "Please keep Rudi with you until I get back."

"I'm going with you," says Yuli.

"No. Rudi will be worried. Just tell him everything is all right. Tell him Bapak is fine and I am bringing him home."

Yuli looks at me.

"Just tell him, please." I reach into my pocket. "Here," I say, handing her the star fruit. "Give him this. Tell him a monkey dropped it—he'll like that."

I leave Yuli in front of our shack and run toward Senen Jaya Metro.

The police station is on the other side of the train station so I have to run back the way I have already come. I keep my head down as I pass Ibu Wangi's shop, but she spies me.

"Why so fast, girl?" she calls out as I run past. "What's the trouble?"

I ignore her and keep running. My legs ache and my chest burns. I push myself on. When I arrive at the police station, there is a lineup snaking its way from the door out to the street. The line is mostly women. I gasp for breath as I join the line, assessing its length. The woman ahead of me looks me up and down.

"Who are you here for?" she asks.

"My bapak," I say. "He was hurt. The police brought him here."

The woman nods. "How long has he been here?" she asks.

I shake my head. "He isn't in jail. The police...they... there was an accident this afternoon."

"Honey, if he's here, he's in jail," she says. "It'll be a long wait. It's visiting day today."

I sway on my heels.

"Do you have water and snacks?" she asks. "Go to the

food stall over there and get something. I'll save your place."
She points to a small stand across the street from the police
station. I am glad for the woman's help. I am thirsty from
running and I haven't eaten since my morning bubur. I buy
a packet of fried shrimp chips and a bottle of water. The
woman's name is Didi. She is waiting to visit her son, who is
being held for stealing a live chicken from her neighbor. He
has been in the police station for two weeks.

"As soon as he gets out I'm going to strangle him," she
says. "I raised him better than to be a thief."

Two hours later, it is dusk and I am at the front of the line.
A tired-looking policeman with spectacles sits behind a
desk. He motions for me to come forward. "Name?"

"Nia," I say.

He looks at me. "The name of the person you are visiting," he says.

"My father. His name is Hendro. He sells fried bananas
at the train station. There was an accident. I think the
police officers brought him here." I pause. "He is hurt."

The policeman studies a list of names. He takes his
time and lights a cigarette. The cloves from his cigarette
spark and crackle as he inhales deeply. "Wait here," he
says finally. He gets up and goes through a door, leaving
me alone.

After a good while, the policeman returns and sits behind his desk. "Your father caused a disturbance at the train station," he says. "It is not permitted to cause a disturbance in a public area."

"He was hurt," I say, talking to my feet. "I want to take him to the hospital."

"There is a fine to pay," says the policeman, blowing thick clove smoke slowly into the air, making my eyes sting. "For the disturbance."

"How much is the fine?" I ask him.

The policeman looks me up and down, seeming to assess how much to ask for. Then he writes an amount on a piece of paper and pushes the paper toward me.

I read the figure and swallow. "I don't have that much," I say.

The policeman smiles and leans back in his chair. "Then you have a problem."

8

Left Behind

I square my shoulders and look the policeman in the eye. "I can give you half that amount," I say. "My father is hurt. I will need money to pay for the hospital."

The policeman is silent. He studies me through the smoke wafting from his cigarette. After a few moments he taps the desk. I guess that means I should put the money there. I take the small roll of bills from my pocket and turn my back. Pulling the notes from the roll, I put the money on the desk in front of the policeman.

He gets up again, slips the money into his pocket. "Wait here," he says.

Once the police release Bapak, we go directly to the hospital. I know he is in bad shape because he leans heavily on my arm and doesn't object when I flag down an Aqua bottled-water delivery truck to take us to the hospital. For a few rupiah the driver lets us ride in the flatbed with the pallets of bottles. Bapak groans the whole way.

Once we arrive at the hospital, we still have to wait a long time before a doctor will see us. All the while, Bapak rocks back and forward moaning in pain from the burns on his hand and arm. His skin looks angry—it is raw and blistering where the hot oil has fried it.

A nurse finally comes and takes him. While I wait, I remember the last time I had been in the same hospital. It was five years ago. We brought Mama here after she gave birth to Rudi at home and the bleeding wouldn't stop. A friend of Mama's, who had helped her through the birth, wrapped Rudi up in a towel and nestled him next to Mama on the stretcher. He was wailing his little head off as they rushed them in. Hours later a nurse brought Rudi back to us.

"Your mama is dead," she said, handing Rudi and a bottle of baby formula to me.

Rudi had stopped crying by then. The hospital nurses had bathed him and wrapped him up in a clean white cloth. I unwrapped the cloth to check him over. He looked beautiful and peaceful. It was like a piece of Mama had been left behind—a piece I could still hold in my arms. I never wanted to let him go.

The doctor who examined Bapak returns and interrupts the flood of memories.

"Your father sustained a large area of second-degree burns," he says. "It will take many weeks for the skin to heal. The nurse will bring him out soon." The doctor leaves me standing in the hospital hallway before a nurse leads Bapak out to me. His hand and arm are bandaged but he looks calm. In fact, on closer inspection, his face has the same slack look it does when he drinks arak.

"I have given your father a painkiller," says the nurse.

"How much will this cost?" I ask her, looking at the bandages.

The nurse has a kind face. "Where do you live?" she asks. "Your father isn't much of a talker."

"By the Senen train tracks."

She nods. She understands.

"The pills for the pain are expensive," she says. "Here, I will give you enough for a few days. You must dress the wounds every day with the ointment and wrap them with clean bandages. Keep the bandages loose and dry." She hands me a package with the pills, bandages, and a tube of ointment to stop the skin from becoming infected.

"Put this package in your pocket. Go to the reception and pay them the consultation fee, but tell them you have no money for medicine."

I open my mouth to thank her, but she shakes her head. "Go," she says. "Go take care of your family."

Bapak is resting on the mattress in our shack. Rudi kneels next to him, holding his hand and patting his shoulder gently. Bapak's eyes are closed, and from the sound of his slow breathing, I can tell he is finally asleep. I check the bandages like the nurse told me to do. The cloth is loose and dry. No doubt it is the pills the nurse gave me that are allowing Bapak to sleep so soundly.

A rooster crows outside, and horns *toot-toot*. The drone of the city is slowly getting louder. Dawn has arrived and I've not had a wink of sleep all night. Neither has Rudi. Yuli told me that he had sat awake, waiting for us to return the whole time.

"Go to sleep now, Rudi," I say. "You can stay home from school today."

Rudi reaches for me. "I don't want Bapak to die," he sobs.

"Bapak is not going to die. Everything will be all right, I promise." Rudi's cheeks are wet with tears. He clings to me tightly.

"Did you know that Dewi Kadita had a pet monkey?" I ask him.

He shakes his head.

"It's true. She used to take him on all her adventures.

He rode on her shoulders and held onto her long seaweed hair like horse reins."

"What was his name?"

"His name was Nero and he could breathe underwater, just like Dewi Kadita. Nero was an excellent swimmer. His favorite food was coconut ice cream."

Rudi giggles and wipes away his tears. "Really?"

"Tell me the whole story," says Rudi. "Please."

I agree and Rudi settles in.

Dewi Kadita was devoted to her pet monkey, Nero. She found him one day in the dusty streets of the market tied up to a tree. He wore a collar like a dog and sat in the branches glaring at the passersby. When people dared to walk too close he would shriek and leap at them, but the rope was not long enough for him to reach them. The rope would yank him back roughly. He belonged to the ice-cream seller who parked his cart under the tree. Nero was the ice-cream seller's star attraction. Children taunted the monkey and threw peanuts at him. Sometimes bad children threw rocks at him instead of peanuts. The children never shared their ice cream with Nero. Sometimes the ice-cream seller gave him the empty ice-cream cups that were thrown in the garbage. Nero licked the cups clean. That's how he knew his favorite flavor was coconut.

One day, Dewi Kadita watched Nero from across the street. To all who passed by, she appeared to be a beggar with leprosy. She recognized Nero's suffering. She waited until the ice-cream seller went for his lunch, and then she walked boldly toward his tree. Nero crouched, ready to shriek and pounce at her. But Dewi held up her hand.

"I am here to help you, monkey," she said. "Let me take that rope from your neck."

No one had ever spoken kindly to Nero before. He sat in the branches and watched as Dewi stood directly under him.

"Come," she said, beckoning him into her arms. "I have a better place for you."

He crawled into her arms and she cut off his rope and took off his tight collar. Then she carried Nero to the ocean. When the monkey saw the giant waves he clung to her in fright.

"Don't worry. You can trust me," she told him.

He wrapped his arms tightly around Dewi Kadita as she plunged into the waves.

Nero was amazed to find himself underwater, but not with a leper beggar after all. He was in the arms of a sea queen. Underwater, Dewi Kadita was beautiful once again. Her green kebaya and long seaweed hair floated around her.

And that is how Dewi Kadita and Nero came to find

each other. Dewi was always devoted to Nero because he had trusted her, even when he thought she was a leper.

"Did Nero ever get to have coconut ice cream?" asks Rudi, sleepy now. His head is heavy against my shoulder.

"Yes. On his birthday they went back to the ice-cream seller," I whisper. "That's how he got his tail chopped off. But that's a story for another day."

Rudi nods before his body finally relaxes into sleep. I curl up with him. A heavy dreamless slumber comes quickly.

9

$\mathcal{S}$tay Sweet

$\mathcal{I}$ wake a few hours later to knocking on the door. Judging from the heat in the room, and the shafts of sunlight peeping through the cracks in the ceiling, it is around midday. Bapak and Rudi are still sleeping on the mattress. I get up to see who is there.

It is Yuli. I put my finger to my lips to warn her to be quiet. I slip outside the door and close it gently behind me.

I am surprised to see Yuli in traditional dress—a batik sarong with a gold sash, and her hair lacquered up in a bun in the old way. We usually dress like this for a wedding or an important ceremony.

"I came to make sure you are all right," says Yuli.

I hug my friend. "I am fine," I say. "You look beautiful. Why are you dressed like this? Where did you get the costume?"

"Tell me first what happened," says Yuli.

"Bapak is hurt. The police beat him and his arm is badly burned. The doctor said he won't be able to work for weeks."

Yuli nods solemnly.

"I will have to take over the cart," I go on. "I will need to take Bapak's place selling the fritters to earn back the money I spent at the police station and the hospital. Rent is due in one week, and I just spent all the money."

"I will help however I can, Nia," says Yuli. "You can count on me."

"Thank you," I say. "I know I can always rely on you, Yuli."

"What can I do?"

"Can you pick up Rudi after school every day and keep him with you until I get back from the market? I can drop him at school early, before I go to the train station."

"Of course," says Yuli. "That's easy. I can get Rudi when I pick up Jojo. The boys can play together until you finish at the market." Yuli takes my hand. "Maybe I can help you earn money," she adds.

"How?" I ask. "What is it? Does it have something to do with the way you're dressed?"

She nods excitedly. "I'm going to get my photo taken by tourists."

"What tourists?"

"Backpackers at the train station on their way to the

mountains in West Java. They love taking photos of girls in traditional dress. They give you money. All you have to do is smile and pose." She frames her face with her hands, arching them upwards in a graceful dancer's posture. Then she pantomimes posing in different postures, blinking her eyes exaggeratedly. "See?" She giggles. "Pretty, pretty. Sweet, sweet."

"Who told you about this?" I ask. "It's dangerous. You're there alone. What if a tourist wants more than a photo with you?"

"Like what? Stop being so bossy. This is a good opportunity." Yuli flaps her hand at me. "Now you really do sound like Ibu Wangi...or my mama."

"Have you told your mama?" I ask her.

"No. Not yet. Anyway, why would it be dangerous? There are lots of people around. Don't worry, silly, it is perfectly safe."

I mix up the batter and drop sliced banana into the mixture before placing the pieces into the fry pan. The fritters bubble as soon as they hit the hot oil. I turn them quickly—once, twice, three times—to get them golden brown on both sides. Once the fritters are ready, I scoop them out of the oil and place them into a paper bag with sugar at the bottom. I shake the bag to coat the fried bananas all over.

"Hot and fresh," I say handing the bag to a teenage boy who is waiting for his order. "The best fried bananas in the entire city." The boy wears a high-school uniform from one of the local schools. "Tell your friends," I say.

The boy bites into his fritter and smiles. "I will," he says, handing me his rupiah. "These are good."

The lunch rush is finally over. I squat next to Mama Tutti under the shade of her umbrella. I wipe the sweat from my face with the hem of my dress. The midday heat is punishing.

Mama Tutti hands me a green banana leaf with a salty duck egg and steamed rice inside. "You'll get used to it," she says opening her copy of the *Flying Gazette*. "Just keep smiling."

After a while Mama Tutti looks up at me from her newspaper. "When you were little, your bapak used to bring along a small plastic chair for you to sit on. He called it the Princess Nia Throne. You would perch there and smile and wave to the commuters." She sounds nostalgic.

"It was my job to sprinkle sugar on the fritters after they were fried," I say.

"Your bapak would say you were his secret ingredient," she says with a chuckle.

I remember it well. It was around that time I had made up my chant: *Flour, sugar, butter, egg...bananas*! Now it runs through my mind from dawn until dusk.

Two weeks have passed since Bapak's accident. His burns are healing slowly, but he is still in a lot of pain. The pills the nurse gave me are long finished. His moods are dark. Each morning he takes the tea and bubur I give him in silence.

I had earned back the money that it cost to bribe the policeman and to pay the doctor. I was able to pay the month's rent. It is a relief. But there is nothing left over after I pay for the staples we need to eat and make the fritters. No rupiah to save for school fees.

"Hit me with some sugar!" A familiar voice breaks into my thoughts. Jimi is a regular customer, a local minibus driver. He rubs his stomach. "I am in the mood for a taste of Nia's sweetness."

I get up from under the umbrella. "Jimi!" I say, waving in greeting. "How is your life today?"

"My life is fine, Nia, just fine," he says. "It will be much better, though, once I have your fritters in my belly." A young man hovers at Jimi's shoulder.

"Nia, this is my friend Alit. He has come all the way from Bali to work in Jakarta. I told him all about your delicious fritters."

I smile hello to Alit as I dip the banana pieces into the batter.

"Are you a minibus driver like Jimi?" I ask Alit.

"Maybe one day," he says. "Right now I am just a conductor. But I plan to work my way to the top, just like Jimi." He slaps his friend's shoulder playfully.

I hand them each a bag of hot fritters. "I put in extra sugar for you."

"Stay sweet," says Jimi, handing me the rupiah for the two bags. "See you soon."

As I push the cart home, my arms feel like lead and my legs ache. For the past two weeks the days have been long—rising at dawn to fetch water, boiling it, making the batter, cooking the breakfast bubur, nursing Bapak's wounds, and getting Rudi off to school—all before I push the cart to the train station in time for the breakfast rush. I am lucky to have Mama Tutti to help me. She shoos away other vendors if they try to set up next to her Tutti Frutti stand before I get there, especially the *martabak* seller. Pancakes and fritters are always in competition for the most popular sweet snack in the market.

I set the cart down by the side of the road to rest my arms. Cavalcades of minibuses speed by and hoot their horns. Motorbikes and scooters weave between vehicles, narrowly missing pedestrians. My eyes burn from the dirt and smoke. Soot from exhaust fumes creeps up my nostrils and clings to my skin, coating me in a film of grime and sweat.

I stand beside a small roadside stall that sells cigarettes, packets of shrimp crackers, peanuts, and bottles of water. I notice there are also spiral notebooks for sale, the same kind that the school provides for homework lessons. I used to write my lessons in tiny letters so that I had pages to spare for my stories.

I reach into the cart for the money box from the fritter sales. I know I shouldn't, but I take out the amount of rupiah for a new notebook and hand it to the stall owner.

"Move along now!" he shouts, motioning for me to get going. "You're blocking my customers."

10

The Bunny Song

Rudi skips and dances next to the cart as we walk home from Yuli's.

"Sing with me, Nia," he says. "Sing with me." Rudi claps his hands. "Let's sing the Bunny Song."

"I'm too tired to sing," I tell him. "Stop messing around. We need to get home."

Rudi ignores my crankiness and jumps up and down as he sings the words:

"Jump, jump, along the street!
Jump, jump, my bunny sweet!
Jump, jump, my bunny high!

Jump, jump, my bunny FLY!"

"Come on, Nia," he says. "Sing with me."

I made up the song for him when he was very small. Before long, I'm singing and jumping along with Rudi. We sing all the way home.

"Jump, jump, along the street!
Jump, jump, my bunny sweet!
Jump, jump, my bunny high!
Jump, jump, my bunny FLY!"

We are still singing when we reach our shack. Bapak is half-sitting, half-lying in the middle of the room, rolling drunk.

"What's this?" I cry. "Why are you out of bed? Where did the arak come from?"

"Keep singing," he slurs. "I want to hear you both sing." Bapak starts to clap, a foolish grin on his face. Rudi is happy to oblige. He jumps around and around Bapak, singing the Bunny Song.

The room is littered with plastic cups, cigarette butts, and peanut shells. I pick up the spilled cups and collect the garbage. There are sticky drops on the floor. The empty cups smell of arak and the whole room smells of stale cigerette smoke.

"Sing with us, Nia," says Rudi, who is now sitting in Bapak's lap. Rudi is beaming, thrilled to have Bapak's attention. Usually Bapak ignores Rudi—silent punishment for his causing Mama's death.

"I am glad you are feeling better," I say to Bapak. "Good enough to have a party."

"My friends take pity on me," he says, stumbling over his words. "They understand I am in pain and need to ease my suffering."

I lift my chin. "How much did it cost, *to ease your suffering*?" I know I am pushing it, speaking to Bapak so boldly. But I am earning the money now and I have a right to know how it is wasted.

Bapak doesn't answer. Instead, he begins to clap again, encouraging Rudi to jump and sing. Rudi looks so pleased that I don't have the heart to keep arguing.

I start to make dinner. I slice some onion, garlic, and chili, and cook it in a frypan with the leftover breakfast rice. I add soy and crack an egg on top.

Bapak continues to sip from his glass as I cook. I noticed his bandages have fallen off, but I feel too crabby and mad at him to fix them.

"Here," I say to Bapak, shoving a plate of fried rice under his nose. "You need to eat."

"Yummy!" says Rudi, grabbing his plate and spooning the rice into his mouth. He spills half of it on the mat. "I love fried rice, Nia."

"You're making a mess," I say. "Settle down and eat properly."

Rudi finishes his bowl and then pecks the fallen rice off the floor. I am too tired to tell him to stop.

Bapak's head lolls. His eyelids are heavy and his half-finished plate begins to slip from his grip. I take it from his hands before it spills.

"Come on, Bapak," I say. "Time for you to go to sleep." I pull on his good arm but he is a dead weight and won't be roused. He slouches over and sleeps where he sits, so I let him be.

I re-dress his wounds and cover him with a sarong.

"Silly Bapak," says Rudi, patting his shoulder. "Sleeping on the floor."

"Yes," I say with a sigh. "Silly Bapak."

Later, once Rudi is asleep and the dinner dishes are washed and put away, I check the old kettle where the money is kept. I unfold the cloth and count the bills. All of yesterday's earnings are gone.

I look over at Bapak's slumped, snoring body. I imagine screaming at him and pounding him with my fists. I swallow my fury and bury my face in my hands.

Exhausted, I lie on the mattress next to Rudi and think of ways that I can stop Bapak from buying arak. My mind races. I know the only way to quiet my thoughts is to write.

I creep out of bed and light the kerosene lamp. I pull out my new notebook. I promised Rudi the story of how Dewi Kadita and Nero got coconut ice cream for his birthday. As always, when my pencil moves along the page, a calm and peaceful feeling settles over me. At least in my stories I can always find solutions to Dewi Kadita's problems.

Ever since the princess saved Nero from his tree prison, the monkey had come to love his underwater life. He spent his new-found freedom riding on Dewi Kadita's shoulders, holding onto her seaweed hair like horse reins as she ruled her watery kingdom. Nero surprised himself to learn that he could breathe underwater and even swim strongly on his own.

On Nero's birthday, Dewi Kadita said, "Come, my dear friend. Let us fetch you some coconut ice cream for your special day!"

Nero had not returned to land since Dewi saved him from being the ice-cream seller's main attraction. The monkey was not too keen to return, but the temptation of eating coconut ice cream was too strong for him.

At the town market, Dewi Kadita and Nero watched the ice-cream seller from across the dusty street. Without his monkey attraction, business was slow for the vendor. The rope that used to be tied around Nero's neck swung loosely from a tree branch.

Nero clung to Dewi's back and hid underneath the old rags the princess wore to cover the leprosy that cursed her on land. They waited patiently until the ice-

cream seller left for his lunch. Then they crept over to the cart and gleefully scooped up as many coconut ice-cream cups as they could carry. Perhaps they got a little carried away, because they took too much and were too slow. The vendor returned and caught sight of his cart being raided. He was enraged to see an ugly leper girl and his very own monkey—both with their arms full of ice cream.

The vendor grabbed a giant machete and held it high above his head.

"Thief!" he yelled.

Nero dropped his ice cream and turned to the vendor, determined to protect the princess. The snarling monkey leapt onto the ice-cream seller's face and clawed and bit him. Soon blood was dripping down the man's face.

"Stop!" Dewi shouted to Nero. "Enough!"

She beckoned Nero and he scampered to her—but it was too late. The ice-cream seller brought down his machete and cut off Nero's tail.

Nero screamed and Dewi Kadita scooped him into her arms. The ice-cream cups scattered to the ground. Dewi ran as fast as she could back to the seaside. Nero was losing blood with every second. People they passed saw only a beggar girl and a tailless, bleeding monkey. No one helped them, not wishing to come into contact with her disease or become tainted by the blood.

By the time Dewi reached the beach, Nero had lost

so much blood he had passed out. Tears dripped down Dewi's pockmarked face as she plunged into the ocean with the dying monkey in her arms. She prayed the waters would revive him in the same way they had cured her of her skin disease.

Dewi swam deep under the waves to her underwater throne, where she lay Nero's lifeless body.

"I am sorry, little one," she wept. "It is my fault. I was foolish to put you in danger. Please, please wake up."

At last Nero began to stir. His eyes opened.

"You are alive!" cried Dewi Kadita.

Nero smiled up at his princess. They were both delighted to find that under the waves Nero's long tail was fully intact.

And at the end of his tail, the monkey held two cups of coconut ice cream.

11

Yuli's Secret

Yuli and I are sitting on the floor in her house. Her mama left at dawn to sell fish at the market. Jojo and Rudi are fighting over who gets to be the fastest minibus driver. They have found rocks that represent the minibuses.

"I am older, so my minibus is faster," says Jojo. "You're just a baby."

"I am not a baby," says Rudi.

Jojo scampers along the dirt floor, making a rut for the rocks. "This is the road," he says. "We have to pick up the people along here. I go first."

"We can smash too!" says Rudi, giggling and crashing

his rock into Jojo's.

Jojo laughs along and they start a new game, slamming their minibus rocks together. Yuli and I ignore them.

"It's getting late," I say, looking out the front door to the lightening sky. "I need to go home and get ready for the market. I have something I need to do before I go to the train station this morning."

"Wait. I want to show you something."

Yuli gets up and retrieves an object from her clothing shelf. She comes back with a money purse. She smiles widely as she opens the purse to show me the contents.

"Look," she whispers.

I peer inside. It is full of rupiah.

"*Wah!* So much money!" I say.

"Shhh!" she whispers, putting her finger to her lips. "Not so loud. I don't want Jojo to hear."

"Where did you get all of that money?"

Yuli does a mock pose for an imaginary camera.

"You made all that rupiah getting your photo taken?"

She nods enthusiastically. "I almost have enough to buy a cell phone."

"Yuli, what are you talking about? If you keep saving, you'll have enough to start high school."

Yuli rolls her eyes and puts her purse away. "That is your dream, Nia. Not mine. I just want to buy a cell phone and some new jeans. Don't you want those things?"

"Yes, of course I do. That's why we need to go to school,

so we can have careers and earn proper salaries."

"I am never going to be able to finish high school. You know that. I'll end up selling fish at the market like Mama. Or if I'm lucky, I'll be a housemaid in some rich person's house." Her voice becomes low. "Or more likely, I'll be sent back to the village to marry some old man."

Two years ago, Yuli's older sister Ania had been married to an older man back in their mother's village. Their mother had arranged it because she was a widow and unable to care for three children alone. Ania is nineteen now with a baby of her own and another expected soon. She spends her days helping her husband in the rice fields, carrying her baby in a sarong. I can't imagine Yuli as a farmer's wife.

I grab her arm. "Stop talking this way. You have as much chance to get an education as I do."

"That isn't true and you know it. I don't have your brains." Yuli shrugs. "Or maybe I just don't have the desire you do. I want to have some fun while we still can. Maybe even catch a bus to Pelanbuhan Ratu. I will buy a ticket for you too. We will walk on the sand and eat fresh coconuts!"

I sit back and study my friend. Something does not seem right.

"How is it that you have made so much money so quickly?" I say.

Yuli looks away. "I told you," she says, not meeting my eyes.

"Yuli! Please tell me you are not doing anything dangerous. Why are the tourists giving you so much money?"

"Shhh!" she says again. "Calm down. I told you, I don't want Jojo to hear."

"Stop avoiding my question!"

Yuli purses her lips together. It looks as if she can't decide whether or not to tell me more.

"Nothing else, I swear," she says finally. "Just posing for photos at the station like I told you."

"But who is helping you?" I ask. "Are there other girls doing this? Do you ever leave the station with the tourists?"

Yuli shakes her head and opens her mouth to answer, but our conversation is interrupted by Rudi's screams.

"He hit me!" Rudi cries. A trickle of blood runs down his forehead.

"The rocks were airplanes," Jojo says.

"But you crashed it into my head!"

Jojo sits on his heels. "See," he says. "I told you that you're a baby."

I try to get Yuli to tell me more, but she busies herself finding a rag for Rudi's head. Before I know it, she is shooing us out the door.

"You'd better go and get a proper bandage on his head," she says. "Go, go—before it bleeds too much."

I am left to wonder. *What is Yuli really up to?*

At home, I patch up Rudi's cut and wrap one of Bapak's

bandages around his head. Bapak is still snoring on the mat. I drop Rudi at school and push the cart toward Jango's arak hut. I force my worry and suspicion about Yuli's earnings to the back of my mind for now. I have a bigger problem to deal with: Bapak and his arak.

As far as I know, Jango's is the only place where Bapak buys arak. Buying home brew can be dangerous, not just because it's illegal, but because it can be mixed with bad chemicals. In the slums we hear about people going blind or dying from drinking bad arak. People stick with vendors they trust.

I hope to convince Jango to stop selling Bapak arak. I am nervous to ask him. No doubt Jango and his friends will laugh at me, or worse. But I have to try.

I arrive at Jango's hut, but it is shuttered up. Perhaps it is too early in the day to sell arak. Jango is likely dead asleep inside. I set the cart down. *It's now or never*, I say to myself.

I pound on the door.

12

Jango's Hut

A little boy who is playing in the dirt nearby looks over at me. "He never gets up until lunchtime," the boy says. "Then my mama brings him some bubur."

"Well, today he is going to get up a little earlier," I say, pounding on the door again. "Go and tell your mama to start cooking."

The little boy remains where he is, likely so he won't miss the sight of Jango rising before noon. He sits crossed-legged in the dirt as if he is ready for a performance. People who were walking by stop as well. Soon a small audience has gathered, all watching in silence as I continue to pound on Jango's door.

"Jango!" I shout at the closed hut door. "I need to speak with you. Open up!"

After a time, the door opens a small crack and the audience applauds.

"What is this?" he asks from inside. "Girl, why are you disturbing my sleep? Get away from here before I come at you." His voice does not sound as fierce as his words. It sounds thick with sleep. I push at the door, opening it wider. Jango is standing with nothing but a sarong wrapped around his waist. The crowd laughs and cheers.

"Scat!" Jango yells at all of us. "Can't a man rest without this foolishness? Go on!" he yells again, waving his arms at the people. "Get going!" The onlookers reluctantly go on their way, except for the little boy who stays glued to his spot.

"Do you remember me?" I ask him.

Jango sighs and looks at me. "What do you want?" he growls. "Tell me what you want and then leave. Does your bapak need some arak? Here, take this. Go."

I push away the cup that he is trying to hand me. "No. That's not what I want."

Jango looks exasperated. He glares at me.

"You knew my mama," I say.

Jango takes a breath and inclines his head slightly, looking at me out of the corner of his eyes. "Yes," he says finally. "I knew your mama."

"You also know that before my mama died, my bapak never came here. You know how different he used to be."

Jango breathes out slowly and stares above my head, but he lets me talk.

"I am here to ask you on behalf of my dead mother to stop selling my bapak your stinking arak."

Jango pulls me inside the hut and slams the door closed. My bravado vanishes and I wonder if he is going to slit my throat for conjuring up my dead mother.

"Do you think I can be responsible for every no-good hopeless low-life scum in this slum?" Jango speaks fast into my ear and jabs the air with his finger to punctuate each sentence. "Listen up, little sister. This life is not fair. This life is not easy. I am sorry about your mama. I am sorry that your bapak has lost his way. But that is not my doing. I make a living any way I can, just like you."

"I thought you would help me," I say angrily, pulling away from him. I hold my nose closed to stop breathing in the foul arak smell that fills the hut.

Jango throws his arms up in the air. "Why? Why would I help you? I am in business to sell, not to turn customers away. I should teach you a lesson, girl." He raises his hand as if to slap me.

"Because my mama told me that she knew you as a boy," I say quickly. "You were from the village next to hers. She said that you were not as mean and tough as everyone said you were." I look from his raised hand to stare into his eyes. "And I remember that you were one of the men who carried Mama's coffin in her funeral procession."

Jango stares down at me. Suddenly he drops his arm. He slumps in a chair and hangs his head, shaking it from side to side.

"Are you hungry?" I ask finally.

Jango looks up.

"I'll make you some fried bananas."

I leave Jango speechless and go outside to the cart. The little boy is still there, standing next to the fried-banana cart. He has one hand on the cart and one with his palm outstretched. "I watched the cart for you," he says. "What do I get?"

I slap his hand away. "You get breakfast," I tell him.

I light the fire and cook two batches of fritters, then I hand one bag to the little boy. "Here," I say. "Take these to your mama, and tell her she can have the day off from cooking his bubur."

The little boy clutches the bag close to his chest and scampers off on his spindly legs.

I carry Jango's fried bananas inside the hut. I hand the hot fritters to him. Jango accepts the bag, reaches inside, and takes a large bite. "You look like her," he says, his mouth full of sugar and banana fritter.

"Who?" I ask.

"Your mama," says Jango. "You look exactly like her." He chews thoughtfully. "You definitely have her fire. She was tough and smart, your mama. We all thought she would be the one to do something special with her life." Jango grinned. "All the boys wanted to marry her. But back then, your bapak, he was the most handsome. He was able to make your Mama laugh."

"So she chose my bapak."

Jango nods sadly. "Yes she did."

That night I dream about Mama.

My head is resting face-up in Mama's lap. She is trickling cool water from the river over my hair. We are together at the river's edge, where the water is crystal clear, and the air smells of frangipani and jasmine.

"You will have to be very clever," Mama says. "You will have to be very strong."

All my worry and sadness wash away in the cool water as I gaze into Mama's face, listening to the melody of her voice and feeling her arms cradle me. I am in such peace being with her again. Her love surrounds me.

"I want to stay here with you," I tell her.

Mama shakes her head. "No, baby," she says. "You still have so much to do."

I look up into Mama's beautiful face. The night sky around her is the deepest of blues—a cobalt blanket littered with sparkling jewels. The jewels are stars, but the stars are all kinds of colors—gold and silver, with ruby and emerald hues that glow like bright gems.

"Is this Heaven, Mama?" I ask her.

She smiles down. "Shhhh," she says. "Rest now."

I relax into her embrace and let time slip away. Calm envelops me. The water is cleansing and soothing. The air is soft and fragrant. I can stay here in Mama's arms forever.

A sound disturbs our peace. Rustling...hissing. *I sit up. I hear it again.* Rustling...hissing. *I don't understand why, but the sounds frighten me.*

"What is that?" I ask Mama. "What is that sound?"

She looks worried.

"It is the giant sea serpent," she says. "It swims up the river from the sea and hides in the caves."

I look around frantically. I see nothing, only darkness.

"Remember," she tells me as she cups my face in both of her hands. "You must remember to be strong. Remember your promise."

I wake up in a sweat with my heart racing. The wind is rattling the tin roof of our shack. I can hear it whistle down the train tracks. I sit up and look around me into the darkness. I am on the mattress with Rudi. He is asleep and breathing deeply.

I feel my head. No water, no river. No rustling or hissing. No sea serpent. It is just the wind. It was all a dream.

I lie back and hot tears spill down my cheeks. I want to dream myself back to that place—back into Mama's arms.

But sleep won't find me again.

13

Charity

It has been two days since I convinced Jango not to sell arak to Bapak. It takes all that time for Bapak to sleep off his last hangover. He finally gets out of bed, but he is sullen and sulky.

"Bapak, your arm and hand are much better," I say as I change his bandages. "The skin is discolored but the swelling has gone. Do you think you will be able to work now?"

He nods without looking at me.

"We have to pay the rent today," I say.

"You go," Bapak says. "It's better if I don't show my

face at the rent office. Not after the police trouble."

"All right," I say. "I will go. But then you will need to take the cart to the market. I have made the batter. Everything is ready."

Bapak remains silent.

"Bapak, we need to make up the money." I hesitate, wanting to say it is because of his arak habit. "We are short of money," I say instead.

"Stop with all your talk. Do as I say," says Bapak. "Go before the line gets too long. Then come and meet me at the market."

"Yes, Bapak," I say, getting up to leave.

Despite Bapak's gruff words, my spirits lift. Perhaps things will get back to normal now. Bapak will soon be fully recovered—he'll return to selling at the market and stop drinking. Then I will focus on my studies again.

I put on my best dress to look respectable at the rent office. I walk through the alleys of the slum, dodging puddles of discarded water, trying to keep my dress and sandals clean from mud and splatter. I reach the busy main road and the endless race of scooters. From where I am standing at the minibus stop, I can see the school across the road. Mr. Surat is out front, unloading bags from a truck. The principal looks up and sees me. He sets down his sack.

"Nia!" he calls, beckoning me. "Come over here. Come."

The last few times I dropped Rudi at school, Mr. Surat asked me to come by his office for a talk. I keep promising him that I will come the next day, and then the next day after that, but I never do. I am always in a rush to get to the train station and start selling fritters.

I have put off Mr. Surat's request long enough. I leave the minibus stop and weave through the traffic to join him.

"What is all this?" I pick up one of the sacks he has unloaded. It isn't too heavy.

"Clothes," he says, hoisting a bag over his shoulder. "Donations from an international aid organization."

"Here," he says. "Help me with these." He hands me two large bags. "There might be something here your size," he adds with a smile.

Mr. Surat and I carry the bags inside, walking back and forth from the truck to his office. I pass one of the classrooms, where the door is slightly ajar. Inside, Rudi catches sight of me. He jumps up and down.

"Nia! Nia!" he cries. "Look! Look!" he says to his friends. "It's Nia!"

I make a face and tell him to *shhhh*. Rudi won't stop jumping around, so I pretend to be a monkey, hopping up and down and scratching my armpits. Soon the entire class is laughing and jumping around like monkeys.

Ibu Merah comes to the classroom door.

"Nia," she says. "I should have known it was you."

"Hello, Ibu Merah," I say, trying to keep a straight face. "I am sorry I disturbed your class."

Ibu Merah narrows her eyes and closes the door. I am familiar with her irritation. Throughout my school years I seemed to easily annoy her with my questions. According to her, a girl like me should not bother her with questions. A girl like me did not need so much information and knowledge. Ibu Merah thinks that girls in the slums will be married off young like our mothers, soon carrying our own babies around. She thinks it's a waste of time for us to be educated. While I was in school, if I asked to borrow a book, she would say that she did not want the library books to get dirty. She often complained that it was her bad luck to be sent to teach in this school, and her wish was to teach somewhere more respectable.

Mr. Surat stands behind me. He shakes his head and laughs. "We miss you around here, Nia."

"I think you are the only one," I say.

Mr. Surat inclines his head with a sad smile. "Come to my office. It's been a long time since we've had a chance to talk."

We enter the principal's office and he motions to the chair opposite his desk.

"How is Rudi doing?" I ask.

"There is no problem with Rudi," he says. "It is you I want to ask about. How are you? Are you keeping up your studies at home?"

"I try," I say. "But I am busy since Bapak had his accident."

"Yes, we heard about it. I am sorry." He pauses. "How is your father? Is he…better?"

"Yes, he is better." I am suddenly worried about what to say. "He is at the market today and I am going to pay the rent."

"You are still not able to register for high school?"

I shake my head. Loyalty to Bapak will not let me say anything more.

"I am sorry to hear this, Nia," he says. "You are a good student. I think you won't be surprised if I tell you that you are the best student we have ever had. You did very well on your examination scores. You could apply for a position at one of the better secondary schools. I would be happy to write a letter of recommendation for you. If you think it will help, ask your father to come and see me. I can explain your opportunities to him."

"Thank you, sir." I study my hands folded in my lap. "I…I will tell my father."

"Nia, I know you have a dream to become a writer one day."

I nod.

"But first you need to attend high school, and maybe after that, you can try for a scholarship," he says. "I hope your father will come and see me soon."

"Yes. I understand. Thank you." I get up to leave,

and bow my head goodbye.

"We miss hearing your Dewi Kadita stories here, Nia. Are you still writing them?"

I nod.

"Will you bring me a new story?" he asks. "The children would love to hear it."

Mr. Surat lets me go only after I promise I will give him a story. I agree that I will send a Dewi Kadita adventure in Rudi's satchel the next day.

I leave by the back door so as not to disturb the kindergarten class again. I recross the road and stand at the minibus stop again. The passing traffic swirls up blankets of dust that sting my eyes.

I don't have to wait long. A bright orange minibus pulls up, pop music blaring from its speakers. The conductor is hanging out of the door smiling and beckoning commuters to step aboard. As I give him my rupiah, I recognize Alit.

"Step up, sweet fritter girl!" he says, helping me up. He points to the empty seats and winks. "Plenty of seats for you, Jimi's friend."

The minibus is half empty, so I take a seat at the back next to an open window. Many other windows are open to try to relieve the hot and stifling air. I sit down and grip the handrail. The minibus bounces up and down over the rough road.

"Enjoy your pothole massage!" Alit shouts above the

music. The passengers chuckle.

A bald man is trying to read the paper but keeps getting thrown around. A few seats ahead of me, two women wearing hijabs have their heads together, talking.

As I bounce around, I think of what Mr. Surat said about my grades. My heart soars and falls at the same time. It was bittersweet to hear that he believes I can earn a place at a good high school and that I could even think of applying for a scholarship one day.

I stare out the window as a swarm of scooters ride dangerously close in an effort to overtake the minibus. I remind myself that Bapak is back at work and that he can't buy arak from Jango anymore. Maybe there is still hope. Maybe if Bapak goes to speak with Mr. Surat, he will help convince Bapak to provide the money I need for school.

I have this thought in my mind when the world suddenly turns upside down.

I am sitting in my seat holding onto the handrail—and then I'm not.

Instead, I am sailing through the air. The sounds of screaming and screeching metal envelop me.

14

A Miracle

My first thought is that my dress is dirty and I will look a mess at the rent office. I spit dirt from my mouth. I look around. My shoulder aches. I am sitting by the side of the road with dust swirling all around me. People are running past me toward the orange minibus. I can hear wailing and screaming. I try to stand up, but my legs feel too shaky.

"Are you all right?" a man leans down and shouts in my ear. "Can you walk?"

I nod and let him help me to my feet.

"Here, let's find a place for you to sit." He leads me to a wooden crate by the side of the road. "An ambulance will be coming soon," he said. "Here, sit. Rest."

I can only nod. I sit down on the crate and try to make sense of the chaos around me. The entire front of the orange minibus has disappeared into the front of another, larger truck. It looks like the big truck has swallowed up most of the minibus. People are staggering around covered in blood. Bystanders are carrying off the two women wearing hijabs. They are unconscious. The man with the newspaper slumps nearby; he has blood pouring down his face.

Then I see Alit lying motionless on the ground. I rise up to go toward him, but someone holds me back, while another lays a jacket over Alit's face.

My mind tries to make sense of what I am seeing.

"The conductor is dead," I hear someone say.

"The truck driver is trapped."

"Impossible for him to have survived the impact."

"The scooters caused him to swerve into the truck."

"No one can see in this dust."

I am in a fog. I hear voices all around me, followed by the wail of sirens, before I realize that someone is shaking my arm. I am not sure how much time has passed.

"Here, let me help you up." A female paramedic leads me to an ambulance. "We will take a look at you. Can you hear me?"

I nod. The paramedic looks in my eyes and ears with a small flashlight. She feels up and down my arms and legs and around my neck.

"How do you feel?" she asks. "Does it hurt anywhere? Does your head hurt?"

I shake my head. I don't want to tell her my shoulder hurts.

"She came flying out of the bus window and landed over there." It is the man again, the one who helped me to sit on the crate. He motions from the minibus to the side of the road. "She landed light as a feather. It was a miracle to watch." He points to the sky. "You must have friends above."

"I do," I say.

"She speaks," says the paramedic. "What's your name?"

"Nia," I say.

"Well, Nia, you are one lucky girl. Not a scratch on you. You're the only who seems to have no injuries."

"It was a miracle," says the man again.

I reach into my hoodie pocket. The rent money is still there, wrapped in the old cloth. "Yes. A miracle," I echo.

"We'll take you to the Gatot Soebroto Hospital so we can properly look you over," says the paramedic.

I shake my head. I have no money for a hospital. It truly is a miracle that I still have the money to pay for the rent. I'm not going to spend it at the hospital.

"I'm fine," I say.

"Do you have someone around here who can take you home? Were you traveling with anyone?" she asks.

I look around to get my bearings. I have traveled north

up Jalan Bungur, but not too far.

"My father works at the Senen Train Station market," I say, pointing south. "I'll go to him."

"I'll walk with you," says the man. "I will return you safely to your father."

The paramedic nods to the man and turns to me. "If you begin to feel any dizziness or headache," she says, "you need to get medical attention, do you understand?"

"Yes," I say.

The man and I watch as the paramedic rushes away to attend a boy holding his arm at a strange angle.

"My name is Oskar," says the man. "It is a pleasure to meet you." Oskar is dressed in a blue suit jacket with a purple tie. His shirt is checked and his pants are shiny light blue cotton.

"I'm Nia," I reply.

Oskar holds out his cell phone. "Would you like to call your father?"

"Thank you, but my father doesn't have a cell phone. And you don't have to walk with me. I'm okay, really." As I hear myself talk it sounds like my voice belongs to someone else, as if I'm in a dream.

"Please. I insist," says Oskar.

People gather around the two smashed vehicles. The crowd is growing as each moment passes. People push and jostle each other to get a good look at the accident scene. It is not unusual for a mob to blindly decide who is to blame for an accident and take its revenge. Sometimes a driver is set alight or beaten. The burned shell of a rickshaw still sits on the edge of the soccer field after a mob attack that happened years ago. The rickshaw driver was accused of trying to swindle a passenger. The mob set his rickshaw on fire and beat him.

Oskar leads me away from the scene. "We should go. Come. It will be my great honor to escort you to safety."

It is a strange thing for him to say, but my head is shaken up from the accident, so I don't ask him why it is an honor to walk with me. Despite what the paramedic said about me having no injuries, I feel like the wind has been completely knocked out of me. Tiny stones are embedded in my palms, and my shoulder aches. I wipe my palms on my dress to get the grit and stones off. Oskar steers me around the chaos. I can still see Alit lying on the ground, his legs splayed out from under the jacket that lies over his face and torso.

"I know him," I say, but my words disappear in the dusty air. I press my eyes shut but I can't erase the image of Alit's body.

We walk south along Jalan Bungur for a short while, and Oskar stays close.

"Slow and steady," he says. "Let's take a shortcut through here." He points toward Pasar Senen, a sprawling six-block shopping area where you can buy anything from brooms to bridal garments. "It will save time," he says.

"Senen Station is on the other side."

I hesitate. I don't know this man and I don't know the shopping area well. Oskar notices my reluctance.

"I am a tailor," he says. "My store is here. I know the way, I promise." He smiles.

Maybe on a normal day I would never agree to walk with a stranger into an area I don't know well, but I am still shaky and Oskar has a pleasant face. I decide to believe him.

"I was waiting for that minibus you were on," he says as we walk. "I saw the whole thing." He shakes his head. "If I had gotten on farther back along the road, I could be dead now." He stares at me intently. "You were the only passenger who escaped unhurt."

Oskar continues to chat the entire way as we wind our way through the shopping stalls. He doesn't seem to expect me to talk back, which is just as well because all I can think about is Alit.

"I was on my way into town to collect some magnificent hand-embroidered silk fabric for a vip client," Oskar is saying. He pronounces VIP like a word, *vip*. "The fabric is special order only. This client has a tip-top position in Jakarta. He entrusts his business attire to me and me alone."

Before too long we have emerged from Pasar Senen to Jalan Senen. We walk along the street toward the train station market. "My father is over there," I say, pointing.

"The fried-banana cart next to the Tutti Frutti stand."

Bapak is sitting in the shade with Mama Tutti. Business must be slow.

Bapak stands as he sees me approach with Oskar. "What happened? Who is this?"

"*This*, my dear sir," says Oskar, holding his palms open to the sky, "is a miracle."

15

Good-Luck Magic

Mama Tutti drags her stool closer to better hear Oskar's account of the miracle.

Oskar recounts the scene with all the flourishes of a stage performer. He has both Bapak and Mama Tutti captivated. It isn't long before people stop to listen as well. Soon a dozen commuters are gathered around, listening to Oskar's repeated description of my flight from the minibus. I notice Ibu Jaga in the small audience. With every telling, Oskar's tale becomes more and more embellished until it sounds like I actually sprouted wings.

"Maybe it was Mama," I whisper to Bapak. "Maybe

Mama saved me."

For the first time in a long while, Bapak looks at me with pride as he used to in the old days. He pats my shoulder. "I am sure it was her," he says. "It's a sign of good fortune."

"It's magic," says Mama Tutti. "Child, you have been blessed with *good-luck magic*."

Oskar nods emphatically. "Yes, magic," he says as his head bobs up and down.

Everyone stares at me. "I was just holding onto the handrail, and the next thing I knew I was sitting in the dirt. It was just luck."

"*Good-luck magic*," Mama Tutti repeats.

Bapak gets up from his stool and addresses the crowd. "Okay, the show is over," he says, his hand on my shoulder. "Please let my daughter rest." He pauses. "Who is hungry for some of Nia's Fried Bananas?" he asks the crowd. "This is Nia herself—my daughter."

A young woman wearing office clothes steps forward. "Me," she says. "But I want her to make them," she adds, gesturing at me. "Maybe some of her good-luck magic will rub off on the fritters."

Bapak looks at me proudly. He raises his eyebrows as if to ask if I can do it.

I nod. It is so nice to see Bapak look at me with pride again.

Luck or magic, what does it matter?

As strange and shaken up as I feel, I know I can cook

bananas fritters with my eyes closed. Besides, maybe if I do something normal I will begin to feel normal. It will take my mind off the sight of Alit's dead body.

I get to work behind the cart, dipping slices of banana into the batter and dropping them into the hot oil. When I look up, the crowd has formed an orderly line. I catch sight of Ibu Jaga in the crowd. She shakes her head as she shuffles away. I wonder why, but I've never had so many customers waiting before, so I forget her. The onlookers are focused on my every move. Feeling self-conscious, I work as quickly as I can while Bapak collects the money.

The last in line is Oskar. He smiles widely and passes some rupiah to Bapak. "No charge," I say, handing him the last bag of fresh fritters. "Thanks for walking me back."

"The pleasure is all mine," he says. "It was an honor." He holds up his bag of fried bananas. "Rest assured I will be telling all my vip customers about you and your magic fritters," he says.

Bapak and I watch Oskar disappear into the crowd.

"We are almost out of batter," I say. "There isn't enough for another batch. We might as well go home." I rub my shoulder where it aches from the accident.

"We will bring the cart home and then I will go to pay the rent," he says. "Where is the rupiah you took this morning?" he asks.

In all the panic, I had forgotten we still needed to pay the rent. I hand Bapak the bundle of money, which I have managed to keep in my pocket the entire crazy day.

"Here," I say. "It's all still there."

Bapak takes the bundle and nods. He puts the rent payment together with the day's earnings. We pack up the cart and I wave goodbye to Mama Tutti. She is still busy serving customers at her fruit stand. Oskar's performance has been good for fruit sales too. She waves back.

"Goodbye!" she calls. "I knew today would be a good day. My right palm was itchy." She holds up her right hand. "It's a sure sign of riches!"

Back at home, Rudi and I wait for Bapak to return from the rent office.

"After I pay the rent, I will buy coconut rice and spicy goat to celebrate," he had told us.

I pressed my lips together, knowing that for him, a *celebration* included arak.

He doesn't know yet that Jango promised not to sell arak to him anymore. He will find out soon enough. What he will do to me when he finds out is another matter.

I remember my promise to Mr. Surat to send a story with Rudi the next day. I take out my notebook. I'm glad to have the blank pages to take my mind off the accident.

The kura kura, sea turtles, gathered before Dewi Kadita—

the Sea Queen, as she was now known—to beg for her help.

"It is the evil sea serpent," they told her. "He raids our nests and eats our eggs. If he is not stopped, we will have no baby turtles. The kura kura will vanish from the seas."

Dewi Kadita sat on her watery throne and listened. Her loyal pet monkey Nero perched on her shoulder.

"We have not wanted to bother you, our Queen," they continued, "but the situation has become grave. We fear for our lives. The sea serpent's greed knows no bounds."

Dewi nodded. "I know the kura kura are proud and noble. I know that you would not have sought my help unless you were in desperate need."

The turtles bobbed their heads and bowed at her feet.

"Leave the problem of the sea serpent with me. I promise you that I will stop him. And he will be punished for his greed."

"Thank you, our Queen," said the kura kura, "but please hurry."

Dewi Kadita told the turtles to go back to their nests and not to worry. She knew exactly what to do.

The queen went to her underwater kitchen and cooked up a delicious platter of sautéed frog legs. She knew the sea serpent would never be able to resist such a juicy treat. She added heaping spoonfuls of hot sam-

bal to the dish and smiled to herself.

Dewi Kadita took the steaming plate of sambal frog legs to the sea serpent's dark cave. Nero threw rocks inside the cave's entrance to get the serpent's attention.

"Sea Serpent!" she shouted. "Come and see what I have brought you!"

The sea serpent took a good long while to appear at the cave's mouth. When he arrived at last, he was irritable.

"Why do you disturb me?" he demanded. "I am busy here with my delicious turtle eggs."

Dewi Kadita and Nero looked away from the horrible sight of the creature devouring the baby turtles alive. The sea serpent's mouth was full of the small turtles. He crunched and swallowed and smacked his lips. "Yum, yum, yum," he exclaimed. "I have more to eat inside."

"You will be glad for the disturbance once you see what I have for you," said Dewi. And she held up the plate of sambal frog legs.

"Fresh and juicy," she said. "I prepared them especially for you."

The sea serpent sniffed at the plate greedily.

"But wait," said Dewi, snatching back the plate. "I put sambal in this dish—maybe too much. Perhaps it will be too spicy for you?"

"Hah!" said the serpent. "Too spicy for me? Nothing is too spicy for me! I can eat more sambal than anyone!"

"No. I see that a bland diet of kura kura eggs does suit you better." Dewi turned to leave. "My apologies for the mistake. I will take the dish to the Octopus King. He enjoys spicy food."

The sea serpent's head darted out from the cave, and he gulped down the plate of frog legs. He swallowed and smiled.

Dewi and Nero watched as the sea serpent began to turn bright red.

"Are you sure you're all right?" asked Dewi. "You look hot."

The sea serpent shook his head, but steam began to seep from his mouth. Soon he began to choke, and Dewi nodded with satisfaction. These were not ordinary frog legs. The bones had been sharpened so they would become embedded in the serpent's throat.

"From now on," she told him, "you can only sip soft seaweed through a straw, otherwise you will choke to death. It is your own greed that has strangled you."

While the sea serpent choked and coughed out sambal fire, Nero scampered into the cave and collected the remaining kura kura eggs. Dewi and Nero left the wailing serpent and took the eggs to the kura kura nest.

Together the queen, her loyal monkey, and the sea turtles celebrated the demise of the sea serpent with plates piled high with spicy goat meat and coconut rice.

16

Charge Double

When I wake up the next morning, I know three things before I open my eyes.

Bapak did not bring home food for us.

Bapak came home drunk.

Life was not going to get back to normal after all.

I know these things because my stomach growls from hunger and I can smell the stench of arak in the shack. In fact, I think it is the smell that has wakened me.

I sit up and look around. Rudi is asleep beside me. Judging by the pale light, it is just turning dawn. My shoulder is stiff and sore. It hurts if I raise my arm too high.

I get dressed carefully and go to the main room. Bapak is there, slumped in a heap with the familiar stink of alcohol wafting from his body. A few discarded plastic bags litter the room. None of the bags have coconut rice or spicy goat in them. They are filled with empty beer cans.

I collect the rubbish, stepping around his sleeping body. One of the bags has a crumpled piece of paper inside. I retrieve the paper and unfold it. The rental receipt is stained with beer but intact. I feel instant relief. At least he paid the rent as he promised to do.

It was foolish to think that asking Jango not to sell Bapak arak would solve the problem. There are arak huts farther away from Jango's, after all, and he can buy beer anywhere, provided he has the rupiah in his pocket—as he did from yesterday's earnings. I guess not bringing food home for us is Bapak's way of punishing me for getting him barred from Jango's.

I clean up the mess while another plan swirls around in my head. I know I can't rely on Bapak to take care of us anymore. I am going to have to take charge of things. I have to at least make sure we keep enough money from the cart sales to buy food and pay the rent. I have to take care of Rudi.

I watch Bapak's sleeping face. The hunger in my belly makes me angry, but at the same time my heart is heavy. I saw a flash of the old Bapak yesterday, but that father had been so quick to vanish. We might as well have buried him with Mama, I decide.

"I'm sorry, Mama," I whisper, "for thinking such an evil thing."

Bapak's jacket is thrown on the floor. I search his pockets for rupiah, but find only a few coins. I go to the kettle. A small stash of money is still there. I stuff the money in my jean pocket.

From now on, if Bapak wants money, he is going to have to fight me for it.

It has been a busy morning. After I collect the water, I go to Ibu Wangi's shop to restock the ingredients for the banana fritters and buy kerosene for the cart stove. I also buy two instant-noodle packets that Rudi and I can have for breakfast.

"That's a lot to manage, girl," Ibu Wangi says, adding up my bill on an old calculator. An electric fan is angled to blow air directly on her face to keep her cool. "I will have Eddie carry it for you." Eddie is Ibu Wangi's helper. He does all the heavy lifting and deliveries for the store. He was a year ahead of me in school.

"Thank you," I say. It is just as well. I put a hand on my injured shoulder. I doubt I would be able to carry the heavy sack.

"I heard about your accident," Ibu Wangi says. "News travels fast around here, you know. I heard that tailor from the shopping district walked you from the accident to the train station. Is he a friend of yours, hm?" She narrows her eyes at me.

I ignore her question. "I am grateful for your help, Ibu. Thank you." I leave before she can ask me anything more.

Eddie hoists the sack over his shoulder and follows me home. When we arrive, I ask Eddie to leave the bag outside the door. I don't want him to come in and see Bapak passed out. Eddie leaves the bag and gives me a nod goodbye.

Once I have dragged the supplies inside, I mix up the batter and boil the water for our noodles. Rudi is uncharacteristically subdued. He eats his noodles in silence, his big eyes on Bapak's sleeping body.

"When did he get home?" Rudi asks me. "Did he bring our coconut rice and spicy goat?" He slurps his noodles thoughtfully, like a miniature old man.

"I don't know," I tell him. "We were both asleep, and there are no signs of any special dinner around here." I decide that I will no longer make excuses for Bapak.

Rudi nods, looking unimpressed.

I try to cheer him up by pouring soy sauce in his noodles, but even this does not change his somber mood. Going to bed hungry is a feeling you do not forget. Rudi is old enough now to understand that Bapak is to blame.

We clean up our dishes in silence and Rudi retrieves his satchel for school. Inside, I place the pages of the story

I wrote last night. "Give this to Mr. Surat," I tell him.

Rudi pauses at the front door and looks back at Bapak asleep on the mat. He turns away in silence and reaches for my hand.

"Let's go," he says.

When I arrive at the train station, the breakfast rush has passed. But at Mama Tutti's fruit stand a line of people are waiting. Oskar the tailor is there too.

"What took you so long?" Mama Tutti cries, running to me. "Hurry!"

"What is this?" I ask. "Hurry for what?"

"They are here for *you*," says Oskar. "They want your good-luck magic. Your good-luck fried bananas. I have been telling everyone about your miraculous escape from death. Everyone wants some of your magic."

I set down the cart and Mama Tutti glances at my supplies. "I hope you made enough batter," she whispers. "You're going to need a lot."

Oskar leans in and speaks into my other ear. "Charge double," he says.

17

Bitter Smoke

When Rudi was a baby, I used to carry him around, wrapped in a sarong sling so he was always cozy and snug. His weight and warmth against me helped to ease the loneliness of losing Mama.

Rudi is on my mind as I dip, fry, and shake bag after bag of Nia's Fried Bananas.

Charging double for the fritters is not cheating, I keep telling myself. I have to do this for Rudi. I have to take care of us. Besides, if it was Mama who kept me safe during the minibus accident, maybe this is her way of helping us? Maybe it really was magic? Who is to say what is luck and what is magic?

Oskar stands close by and continues to tell the customers the story of the supposed miracle. The lineup for fried bananas does not stop, and most people didn't flinch when I charge double the regular amount—except for a few regular customers who aren't too happy about the cost and my new popularity.

"Nia, these are the same fried bananas I have bought every week for years," says Samir, the ticket seller from the train station. "Where is your father? Why do I suddenly need to pay more?"

What can I say? That Bapak is at home, passed out? That I am charging double because I am magic? I keep quiet and hold my hand open for the money.

"Move on, man!" a waiting customer shouts at Samir. "We're all waiting here!"

"I'd just as well save my money," says Samir before he stomps off.

I may be losing some old customers, but new ones keep lining up. By lunchtime, I already need to make more batter. With Oskar broadcasting the miracle story, the line is constant. Some customers want to know how long I have been magic, or if I was born that way. Others watch me intently like I am a rare bird that might flap away any second.

"What did it feel like to fly from the bus?" someone asks.

"Can you put extra magic in these fried bananas?"

asks a pretty woman with dangling earrings. "I am going to take them to my son. He has been sick." The woman smiles at me with such hopeful enthusiasm that I find myself nodding back. Her expression masks a look of sadness and exhaustion. "I am sure your good luck will cure him," she says.

I hand her the bag of fritters. "Best of health to your son," I say.

I am leading people to believe I can somehow change their fortune. But the rupiah keeps pouring in. I have already made more money in a single morning than any full day before. If it keeps up, I could have my school fees saved up in a few weeks.

The woman with the dangling earrings leaves with her fried bananas. I am surprised to see that Big Sula's mother is next in line. Her hair is lacquered in a giant bun. The bun looks so stiff that it must have taken a whole can of hairspray to hold it.

"Hello, Nia," she says, her eyes darting around. She looks at me, then at the fritters, and back at me again. "I heard about your accident. I am so glad you are okay. When I heard about it, I told my customers that the magic minibus girl is a friend of my very own daughter. To think, we've had a good-luck charm living among us all this time."

Big Sula's mama doesn't expect the good-luck charm to speak back.

"Can you cook a bag of Nia's Fried Bananas for Sula?" She hurries on. "She has an exam this afternoon. I know she will do extremely well with your good luck."

There is not a fritter in existence that will help Big Sula with her exam scores, I think as I drop the bananas into the hot oil. I turn the fritters over and over in the oil, wondering what it would be like if your only concern was to study and do well on your exams—if you didn't have to worry about food or rent, or your father drinking up all the money you do earn.

Or if you still have a mother and she stands in a long line to buy you fritters.

I flip and flip Sula's fried bananas until I realize the fritters are almost burning. Bitter smoke starts to rise from the oil. I scoop them out just in time as they turn a dark golden brown. I drop them into the sugar bag and give them a rough *shake, shake, shake.*

"Say hello to Bi—I mean, say hello to Sula," I say.

"Oh, I will Nia. I will. And I will let you know her exam scores."

As I watch Big Sula's mama's bun float away above the crowd, I catch sight of the martabak seller scowling at me from his pancake cart. I smile to myself. Today, at least, I've come out on top in the pancake-fritter war.

On the way home I pass Jango's hut. I am across the street, so unnoticed I look around to see if Bapak is hanging around outside. What I see instead makes me rub my eyes. It is Yuli. She is dressed in her traditional costume again and she is coming out of Jango's door. Jango stands at the doorway behind her. He appears to slip something into Yuli's hand before she turns to go. I open my mouth to call out to her but the words stick in my throat. I feel I have seen something I shouldn't have.

What business does Yuli have with Jango?

18

Nightmares

A few days later when I go to pick up Rudi, Yuli's mama stands grimly in the doorway.

"Your father said he needs to go back to his family village in Lembang to see about his land," she says. "He said to tell you to take care of Rudi and the cart, and that he will be back soon."

"Look, Nia!" says Rudi, coming to the door to show me a smooth black stone. "Bapak gave this to me. He said I should take care of it until he gets back from the country. He said that he will build us a new house by that river you always talk about. The clean river with the jasmine flowers."

I try to return Rudi's smile, but I can't. I look at the stone, passing it from one hand to the other. My head is swimming with the news that Bapak has left. Since my accident he has been mostly absent, but leaving the city is completely different. He would drop by the market from time to time to take the money from the banana sales, but he never stayed long enough to help with the cart. "The customers want you to serve them, not me," he would say before disappearing again. Once or twice I saw him in deep conversation with Oskar.

Rudi grows impatient and snatches the stone back. "It's mine," he says. "I need it back now."

I thank Yuli's mama for watching Rudi. "When will Yuli be home? I need to talk to her."

Yuli's mama shrugs. "Who knows? She is never home these days." Then she grips my arm tightly. "Listen. Don't tell anyone that you are alone. It will be safer if no one knows."

I swallow. A fresh fear is taking root in my stomach.

On the walk home, Rudi is full of excited chatter. He has forgotten about Bapak lying passed out on the floor. He believes Bapak is building us a house in the country. Since Rudi was a tiny baby, I told him all the same stories and dreams that Mama told me. The difference is that now I know they are just that—dreams, not real. Bapak doesn't have enough money in his pocket to buy rice for a week, let alone a house. I am not sure where he has gone or what he is doing, but I know he isn't building us a house by a mythical river.

"Jojo doesn't have a stone like this," Rudi says. "Bapak only gave one to me. I'm going to keep it safe so I can take it with me when we move to our new house very, very soon."

I don't correct Rudi. I don't want to stomp all over his dream. When we arrive home, I am relieved to find everything is still in its place. Only some of Bapak's clothes are gone. The chest with Mama's things is still there—even her gold wedding comb. It gives me the tiniest hope that maybe what he said to Yuli's mama is true, that he will return soon.

After dinner Rudi plays with his stone and I count the day's earnings. It is more money than ever before. If I keep selling fried bananas at this rate, I will have enough for food and rent, with money to spare. If I keep charging double, I can save rupiah for school. But even if I save enough money, if Bapak stays away, there will be no parent to sign the registration form. And who will earn our rent and food money, and care for Rudi? I am fooling myself with hope that I will ever attend high school. I am fooling myself to think that I will ever have a life outside of this slum and the fried-banana cart.

The thought makes me feel mean-spirited.

Rudi is balancing the smooth stone on the back of his hand. "How long will it take for Bapak to build our house and come for us?" he asks, his eyes focused on his game.

"Maybe never."

Rudi lets the stone drop into his palm.

"Rudi, I have to tell you something. Sometimes grown-ups lie. Sometimes they go away."

"Don't say that!" Rudi glares at me. "Bapak told *me* he was building us a house, not you."

"I know what he said, but he—" I stop. What is the point of scaring him with my fears?

"Let's just hope he gets back soon," I say instead.

"Is there arak in the village?" asks Rudi.

"Maybe," I say. "I don't know."

Rudi puts the stone on the ground in front on him and scowls at it.

Later that night, once we are in bed, Rudi wants to hear the story of when Dewi Kadita tricks the sea serpent with sambal frog legs.

"Start at the beginning," he says, "when the turtles ask for her help."

I only reach the part when Nero throws rocks into the serpent cave when I hear Rudi's heavy breathing and know he has fallen asleep.

I close my eyes and hope that I will visit Mama again in my dreams, and that she will tell me what I should do. But I have a nightmare about the minibus accident instead.

People with blood dripping down their faces are crowding around the fried-banana cart. Alit is at the front of the line, waiting to buy my fried bananas. But the fritters are burning in the oil. Bitter, black smoke rises from the pan and drifts around his face.

"Bad deeds burn easily," he says. "You should beware, or you'll be telling your good-luck-magic lies to demons and sinners."

19

Men's Business

Oskar the tailor takes to flapping around the fried banan-as cart like a proprietary rooster.

Mama Tutti, who at first treated Oskar like a favored son, is starting to show irritation at his hovering presence.

"It looks like business is excellent, ladies, excellent," says Oskar, rearranging bags of cut-up mango on Mama Tutti's fruit table. "I have told all my vip customers about this once-in-a-lifetime opportunity of eating fritters cooked by a true magical being—and look!" Oscar points to the lineup. "Success!"

Mama Tutti slaps Oskar's hands away from her fruit

display and makes a kind of slow hissing sound out of the side of her mouth.

"It is surprising that you have so much time to spend here when you must attend to your 'vip' customers." Her lazy eye starts to twitch.

"It is true, my dear Madame Tutti, I am a busy fellow. But I feel it is important to continue showing my support where it is needed," replies Oskar.

Mama Tutti shooes flies away from her pineapples and stares him down with her good eye. The other one jiggles spiritedly. She places her body like a barrier between Oskar and her produce. Oskar sensibly steps away and stops trying to reorganize her fruit.

When the mood strikes him, Oskar entertains the fritter customers with his fanciful story of my flight from the crashed minibus. He has become fond of ringing the cowbell. As embarrassing as it is, there can be no denying that he is very good at drumming up business and justifying my high price for fried bananas.

Oskar sidles up to me as I am taking a customer's rupiah. He gazes at his cell phone importantly, then fixes his eyes on me. "I see you are still charging a healthy amount for your fritters," he says. "And with good reason. This is a once-in-a-lifetime opp—"

I cut him off. "Yes, you keep saying. But you can see we are busy right now."

"I understand, sweet girl," he says. "I do. But I would

like to speak to your father. He hasn't been here for the last few days. You keep saying he will return soon, but so far I have not seen him." Oskar pauses and seems unable to drag his eyes away from the rupiah in my hand. "I have important matters to discuss with him."

I have stalled Oskar for the last three days, not willing to confess that Bapak has left the city. But I now realize that Oskar is not going to be deterred so easily. I will have to come up with a different excuse for Bapak's absence.

"He has urgent family business to attend to," I say, trying to sound professional. "Maybe you can discuss what you want with me instead. I will communicate it to him."

"I don't wish to trouble you, my dear," he says. "Besides, these are men's concerns. Nothing to bother you with...at least not yet."

"Come back in two days then," I say. "He should be back."

Oskar sighs. "As you wish," he says. "But perhaps when he returns, I will visit your father in your home? I know where you live."

He does? I wonder how he knows where we live, but I am busy mixing up a new batch of batter. Oskar wanders a few paces away and starts in on one of his retellings, although it lacks his usual gusto.

I notice Ibu Jaga crouched in the shade of the adjacent awning, listening to Oskar. Occasionally her eyes dart to me. The old woman looks to be having a break from sweeping graves. Her long reed broom lies at her feet. She stares at Oskar, then at me, and back again. She shakes her head each time.

"Do you know her?" I ask Mama Tutti, inclining my head toward Ibu Jaga. Mama Tutti cranes her neck to see.

"Of course," she says. "Everyone knows Ibu Jaga. She tends the riverside cemetery." Mama Tutti pauses and a shadow passes across her face. "She has had a difficult life."

"Do you think she is hungry?" I ask.

"Best leave her be," says Mama Tutti. "She is proud. She can take care of herself."

"She looks scary."

"She is not scary. She is just old. Leave her be."

Perhaps I am tired of Ibu Jaga's scornful expression and hope to win her over. I don't know. But I am willing to put aside my usual fears to find out. Maybe I have started to believe I'm really magic.

"I'm going to take her some fried bananas," I say.

Mama Tutti shakes her head. "Suit yourself. But I doubt she'll want them."

I ask my next customer to wait and I approach the old woman.

"Hello, Ibu," I say, holding out a bag of warm fritters. "Would you like some fried bananas?"

Ibu Jaga assesses me coldly. She wears a dusty head-scarf and is missing many of her teeth. A ragged scar slashes down the side of her cheek and disappears into her scarf.

"Keep your fried bananas," she says, flapping her hand at the flies buzzing around her eyes. "I have no stomach for them."

"You don't like fried bananas?" I ask her.

She grunts. "I like fried bananas fine," she says as she eases herself up from the ground slowly.

"Maybe you don't remember me. I am Nia. I used to come to the cemetery with my mother." I hold my hands together to meet hers in the traditional way of greeting.

"I know who you are," she says, and spits on the ground at my feet. Then she shuffles away without meeting my gaze.

Still holding the fritters, I turn back to Mama Tutti.

"See?" Mama Tutti rolls her eyes at me. "What did I tell you?"

20

Losing Friends

I sit on the mat in Yuli's house. It has been a while since we've had a chance to talk. I look over at Rudi, who is wrestling Jojo on the floor.

"You're famous, Nia. Everyone is talking about your magic fritters."

"Luck or magic," I say. "Whatever it is, it's helping me to make good money."

"Hah!" Yuli laughs. "So now you don't mind a little mumbo jumbo, huh? What happened to 'Yuli, don't believe in those silly supernatural stories in the *Gazette*'?"

"This is different."

Yuli raises her eyebrows. "Why?"

I bite my lip, not finding words to reply.

"Anyway," Yuli continues. "I'm just glad that you were not hurt and that your fritters are popular. Especially since your bapak has…"

"It's okay. You can say it." I shrug. "Gone."

Yuli reaches for my hand. "I'm sorry."

"For now I just have to focus on taking care of Rudi and keeping us safe."

"From what?" asks Rudi, slipping from Jojo's choke hold. "Safe from what?"

"Nothing," I say. "Mind your business."

Rudi shrugs and dive-bombs Jojo. The boys continue to roll on the floor in a jumble of intertwined arms and legs.

"I'm sure your bapak will be back soon," whispers Yuli.

We study one another in silence before Yuli looks away.

"Yuli," I say, my voice low. "Tell me why I saw you leaving Jango's hut the other day."

Yuli goes bug-eyed and scrunches up her face. "Don't be mad."

"Just tell me. Does this have something to do with all the money you're making?"

She nods but stays silent.

"Okay, so…tell me," I prod.

Yuli fidgets with her long hair and twirls it around her finger. She looks out through the open doorway.

"The traditional costume and photos are just a cover,"

she says finally. "A way to...a way to ask the tourists..." She pauses again. "A way to ask if they want any *ganja*."

I slap my hand over my mouth.

"And if they do," she goes on, "I get the ganja from Jango and deliver it back to them. Jango gives me a fee."

"So it was Jango's idea all along? The photos? The ganja? Did he give you the costume?"

She shrugs. "He asked if I wanted to make some money and I said yes. He didn't force me to do anything." She grips my arm. "Nia, I am glad for it! Now I have money of my own to do what I like. I can buy new clothes and food for mama and Jojo. And I have almost saved enough for a cell phone."

"But it isn't safe," I say. "If you are caught, you will go to jail. Don't you remember when Arjun's brother got caught with ganja? He was sent to jail! He's still there."

"That was different. He was in a gang and he was doing other things besides."

"You have to stop."

Yuli narrows her eyes at me. "Stop?" she says. "Nia, sometimes I wonder if we live in the same world. You spend too much time with your Dewi Kadita fantasies." She continues to glare at me. "Why would I stop? I'm making money the only way I can, just like you are. Who are you to tell *me* what to do? You think because you are suddenly 'magic' that you're better than me? That you can tell me what to do?"

I am shocked by Yuli's sudden anger. I have never seen her so mad.

"I'm...I'm just worried about your safety, that's all."

"Well, worry about your own safety, not mine." She gets up from the mat. "You should go now. I need to get ready."

She turns her back as we leave. For the first time in our long friendship, we don't say goodbye.

Weeks pass in a blur of frying fritters and batting away questions from nosy customers about my special powers. All the while Oskar hovers over my shoulder. The less I say the more people seem to believe I am magic. And while I am still making money, I won't deny it.

"Can you walk through fire?" a young boy asks as he waits for his fried bananas. I shrug and look sideways. The boy takes this as a yes and gleefully grabs his fritters before running off to tell his friends.

I hear a familiar voice call my name. It is Jimi.

"Hello, Jimi," I say. "It's good to see you. It has been a while."

Jimi does not wear his usual bright smile. "Yes, it has been a while. I hear your fritters are now too expensive for your old customers."

A flush begins to creep across my cheeks.

"Is it true? That you're charging double because the fritters are meant to give customers some kind of magic? I couldn't believe my old friend Nia would do such a thing,

146

so I thought I'd come and see for myself." Jimi peers over the cart at some freshly fried bananas. "They look like the same fritters I've always bought from you. Nia, why would you choose to profit from a terrible accident in this way?"

Jimi watches my face get redder and redder as he waits for me to answer. I chew my lip.

"You were very lucky that you were not harmed in that accident, and I am glad for it," he says. "But there was no magic."

"Did you see the accident? How do we know what is luck and what is magic?" I ask him, finding my voice. "Were you there, Jimi?"

"No, I didn't see it." Jimi pauses. "But Alit died in that accident, and he was my friend."

I cast my eyes down, shame making my heart drop. I remember Alit lying on the ground with a jacket covering him. I remember him in my nightmare.

"I know. I am sorry," I say, my voice beginning to break.

"I have been in Bali with his family these past weeks. I am trying to help the family prepare for his cremation and take care of his younger brothers. Alit's mother is a widow. He was supporting the whole family."

I try to dispel the image of Alit's dead body.

"Please tell Alit's mother that I am sorry for her loss," I say. "And that I will remember him in my prayers."

"I'll do that, Nia. You were one of the last people to see him alive."

An image of Alit comes to me, smiling and swinging from the minibus door, encouraging passengers to step aboard.

"He made a joke," I say. "About a pothole massage. He made us all laugh."

Jimi half-smiles. "He liked to do that, to make people laugh. His family will be glad to know that. It will mean a lot to them."

The customers lined up behind Jimi are growing impatient. I want Jimi to stay, to keep talking, to be my friend again, but he turns away. I wait, hoping he will say, *Stay sweet, Nia*, like he always does. But he just holds up his hand as a goodbye and disappears into the jostling market crowd.

First Yuli and now Jimi. Yuli still won't speak to me. She is never home when I pick up Rudi after the market, and she doesn't stop by our shack like she used to on her way to fetch water. When I ask where she is, her mama makes up bad excuses like *Yuli is visiting her aunty*, or *Yuli is buying rice*. I can tell Yuli's mama is lying because she will not meet my eyes.

Throughout all my worries, Yuli has always been there for me. We listened to each other's problems. We washed each other's hair. We knew each other's dreams.

I have lost my best friend.

21

Shame on You

The next day, Mama Tutti is visiting relatives in Surabaya, and I am alone when Big Sula's mama comes striding up to the cart.

"It didn't work," she says. She stares down at me, her face sweaty. "Sula failed her exams. She received the worst score she has ever had!"

I gaze at Big Sula's mama and wish I could be the one to sit the exam instead of her mean daughter.

"I want my money back." She smacks the cart with her palm.

I reach silently into the money box and take out the

rupiah. I place the money in her hand.

"You're a disgrace," says Big Sula's mama, clutching her rupiah as she turns to leave. "Shame on you."

Big Sula's mama tells other customers at the market that I gave her back her money. The news travels fast. Some people come and ask for a refund, but others insist that it will be bad luck to take their money back.

"The magic will get offended," says a t-shirt vendor. "It will turn into bad luck instead." He is a walking display for his garments and wears many layers of his t-shirts. He's a regular customer of the magic fritters, hoping they will increase his sales. "A sound business investment," he always says before gobbling up yet another fried banana.

Others think it's only patience that is required.

"You just have wait for the good luck to find you, that's all." It is the pretty woman with the dangling earrings and the sick child. "Keep your money, sweetheart," she says to me. "I still want to believe in your good-luck magic."

Big Sula's mama's loud complaints cause the fritter sales to dwindle. For the first time since the accident I don't have a lineup at the cart.

I am collecting the garbage that's scattered around—mostly paper bags, peanut shells, and cornhusks—when Oskar comes running up to me.

"What is this?" He stands erect in his bright red jacket, gesturing to the empty space in front of the fried-banana cart. "Where is everyone?"

"A customer complained that the magic didn't work," I tell him. "I had to return money to some of them. Maybe they are right. Maybe it wasn't magic that saved me in that accident. Maybe it was just luck."

"No! It *was* magic. I saw it with my own eyes." Oskar looks around frantically, ready to launch into one of his performances, but the market crowd just pushes by him.

"Even if it was a miracle, it was only meant for *me*. it's not mine to give to anyone else. Not one person has told me about having good luck from eating my fritters." I stare at him. "Why do you even care? I am grateful to you for helping me that day. But, please, go back to your shop and your *vip* customers. Leave me alone. I don't want to pretend I am something I am not anymore."

"Where is your father?" he asks. "You keep saying he will return, but it has been a long while. I told you before that I have business with him."

"He is gone!" I shout.

Oskar pulls back like I have slapped him.

"See? I am not special. I am not magic. I am just a normal girl with a temper who doesn't have any parents." I throw the garbage I've been holding at his feet. "If you have any business to discuss, it is with me."

"Your father is gone? What do you mean *gone*?"

"He left us. I am on my own. So like I said, if you have any business to discuss, it is with me. There is no one else."

Oskar peers at me. "You are really all alone?"

"Please just go."

Oskar nods his head rapidly. "I see. I understand." He retreats into the crowd and rushes off without another word.

I clean up the garbage again and close up the cart. All the while, Ibu Jaga glares at me from her spot under the awning. She has been listening, and from the look on her face, does not like what she hears.

The list of people who are upset with me is getting longer and longer.

I think more about what I said to Oskar. It is true. No one has reported good-luck magic from eating my fritters. Jimi is right. What happened was luck, not magic. It is time to stop.

"Do you think you are better than us?"

It is the martabak seller. He stands in front of the cart, blocking my path as I try to leave the market. "I heard that your customers asked for their money back. You're a cheat. First you say you are magic. Then you charge double for this so-called good-luck magic. Now you think you can just leave without paying your debts?"

The anger in his voice and the hatred in his eyes make my heart race.

"I—I'm sorry," I say. "It was wrong. I didn't mean to make trouble. I—"

"You are a thief and a liar," he says. He moves closer to me and points his finger between my eyes. "Thief!" he says louder. Now he is shouting. "THIEF!"

A crowd starts to gather around us. They watch intently as the martabak seller keeps yelling that I'm a thief. I look from one face to the next. Cold eyes stare back at me. They are deciding if he is right.

I try to push past the martabak seller, but he grips the end of the cart and will not let me pass. The crowd encircles me. I swing around, searching the faces for someone familiar—Jimi, or one of my regular customers. I would even be happy to see Oskar. But they are all strangers.

"She thinks she can trick everyone," the martabak seller is saying. "She thinks she can steal people's money. She thinks she can pretend to be magic, like a witch."

"No, I don't," I say. "Please, you don't understand…it has all been a mistake. I-I have tried to pay people back."

"It's too late," he says. "You are a thief and a liar. You need to be punished."

More onlookers join the scene, pushing and shoving to get a better look at what is happening. In mere minutes the crowd has become a mob. The martabak seller now has a rock in his hands. I can see others picking up stones and objects. I know it will only take one person to throw something before others join in.

"Please…no, please…" I can hear my voice shake.

The first rock hits the cart with a crash. I duck and crouch behind the cart, holding my arms over my head. More objects smash into the cart and my back. The martabak seller shouts to the mob to punish me. They pelt me with stones and garbage. I have to get away. But the angry people keep circling in closer and closer. I glance up, but can only see a blur of faces. The mob wants blood. Their eyes are glazed with excitement. They want to punish me.

Then I feel cold liquid poured over me. It smells of kerosene. Someone has tipped the fuel from the cart all over my head. Panic grips me.

I stand up. "No!" I shout, spinning around. "No! No! No!"

The mob steps back, startled that I'm on my feet. A hush descends as I stagger around, looking for a way out. All I can see is a wall of bodies. Frantically I search the circle of faces again, hoping for a sign of compassion.

"Please," I beg. "Please help me!"

The martabak seller takes out his lighter and holds it up for everyone to see.

"We know the punishment for thieves and liars," he says.

The mob watches silently. No one speaks. The kerosene stings my eyes and burns my skin. Each second feels like an eternity. I keep searching from face to face, as I implore them for mercy. No one meets my gaze.

"First she tells you she is magic and then she steals your money," says the martabak seller. The crowd murmurs in agreement. "A liar and a thief!"

"STOP!" A voice shouts from behind the crowd.

The people turn to see who it is. A woman is pushing her way to the front. She reaches the martabak seller and snatches his lighter.

"Shame! Shame on all of you!" she cries hoarsely.

It is Ibu Jaga. She stands in front of me, shielding my body as she points her finger and glares at the crowd. "You all know this child. She is one of you. It's true she has been foolish, but would you hurt her? It is not up to you to judge her. That is for God only. Shame on all of you!"

"It's Ibu Jaga, the keeper of the cemetery," someone in the crowd says. "We'd better not anger her. I don't want to risk my fate with a gravekeeper." Others mutter and look around anxiously.

The mob disbands and melts back into the market. The martabak seller grabs his lighter back from Ibu Jaga and stomps away.

As quickly as it grew, the murderous mob is gone.

I fall to my knees and sob.

22

Right and Wrong

"Come now, girl," says Ibu Jaga, and she bends down to help me to my feet. "We must get you cleaned up."

We leave the cart where it is and Ibu Jaga leads me away from the market. I stumble as we enter the train station. People stare at us but keep their distance. I reek of kerosene. My skin and eyes burn from it. Ibu Jaga leads me to the public washroom. She gives the attendant some coins and the woman lets us enter. Once inside, Ibu Jaga points to the last stall. It is a shower cubicle. A nozzle is attached to the tiled wall and it has a single cold tap. She buys a handful of shampoo packets from the attendant.

"Take off your clothes," Ibu Jaga instructs. "Use this for your hair." She hands me the shampoo. "Keep washing until your hair squeaks."

I turn on the tap and a stream of clean water pours from the nozzle. The cool water relieves my burning skin and washes away my tears. The apple fragrance of the shampoo is a salve against the pungent oil. I say a silent prayer of thanks that the cart's kerosene canister had only been a quarter full.

Ibu Jaga comes into the stall and hands me a dry t-shirt and a sarong. "Put these on now," she says. Her manner is rough but her kindness brings a lump to my throat. She is the last person I ever imagined would help me.

"Thank you," I say, taking the clothes. My legs are still trembling. "Y-you saved me. I don't know what would have happened—" Ibu Jaga waves away my thanks.

"Just get dressed," she says.

As I dry myself with the sarong, Ibu Jaga speaks again. "Many years ago, when I was barely older than you, a gang of men hurt me—angry men like the ones you saw today. These men had the notion they would be cleansed of their sins if they took a young woman's innocence. This is one of the many ignorant superstitions peddled to justify evil behavior."

She lifts her headscarf to show me the ragged scar that runs across her face.

"As if that wasn't enough, they took a trophy as well."

The scar ends where Ibu Jaga's ear should have been.

"You learned today that lies and superstitions cause pain." She rewraps her headscarf and looks me square in the eyes. "You are fortunate that you did not see a worse fate."

"I-I didn't mean to hurt anyone," I stammer. "It's what people wanted at first...was that so wrong?"

Ibu Jaga grunts. "You know the difference between right and wrong. Sometimes telling a lie is the right thing; most times it is wrong. Sometimes superstitions are harmless, other times they hurt and deceive people." She drills her bony finger into my chest. "You decide, in here, what is right and what is wrong.

"Now," Ibu Jaga adds, "you need to get your cart before someone steals it."

We go back to the market to retrieve the cart. It stands alone, looking sad and beaten.

The money box is empty. During the ordeal I did not think to protect it. My rupiah is surely now in the pockets of my attackers. I collect the utensils scattered around on the ground before lifting the cart handles and pushing it toward home.

Ibu Jaga walks with me slowly along the train tracks. My mind struggles with what she told me about her assault and the truth of how narrowly I escaped real harm. I try to add up in my head how many coins I owe her for the shampoo and the clothes, but my brain will not hold numbers. Instead, my mind keeps falling back to the faces of the angry people.

I need to be distracted. "Ibu, tell me how you came to be caretaker of the riverside cemetery," I ask her. "Will you tell me your story?"

When Ibu Jaga was a young girl, she tells me, her name was Danita. She lived with her parents on a large tea plantation in Bogor, originally owned by a Dutch family. The Dutch had occupied Indonesia for hundreds of years, but in 1950, the year Danita was born, Indonesia regained its independence. The Dutch owners were forced to leave, but a wealthy family from Jakarta took over the estate. Danita's mother stayed as the cook, and her father became the caretaker.

Every morning at dawn, Danita's father would begin his rounds of the property. A family of macaques lived close by. The monkeys' home was a riverbed lined with acacia trees. One of the father's jobs was to scare away the monkeys if they ventured too close to the big house. When Danita was five, her father permitted her to accompany him on these early morning rounds. Her mother would give them both hot sweet tea and fried plantains before they set out.

Danita loved the fresh coolness of the morning air and the smell of damp grasses and wild passion fruit vines.

Sometimes they would crouch beside the river and watch the macaques' morning grooming ritual. The little monkey babies clung tightly to their mother's bellies and pulled faces at each other, while the older monkeys sat behind one another, patiently picking and smoothing out each other's fur. The grooming was a long and unrushed process, but Danita never tired of watching them. Often her father would leave her by the river to watch the macaques while he completed his rounds. He always came back with something he had found for her—a ripe mango, a warm, blue duck egg, or fresh banana leaves for her mother to wrap up with their steamed rice for lunch.

As a child, Danita was not aware that she was poor. She just knew her life as it was, living with her parents and playing with the other children who also lived on the tea plantation.

Everything changed when a group of vigilantes came to rob the estate. The vigilantes did not just want to rob the family. They wanted to punish the wealthy. They wanted blood. Among the many dead that night was Danita's father.

Danita and her mother continued to live on the property until her mother died of tuberculosis six months later. By then, Danita was thirteen years old. Perhaps fearing Danita also carried the disease, the owners threw her out.

"But why should I tell you about the difficult years that followed?" Ibu Jaga says. "What purpose would it serve? Who wants to remember such hardship? I was already an old woman when I found my place at the cemetery by the riverbank. I finally found peace and a place where I could be a caretaker, just like my father."

We walk the rest of the way together in silence. Ibu Jaga leads the way as the alleys narrow. Somehow, she knows where she is going through the maze of paths to our shack.

She stops once we reach my door.

"Did you leave your place unlocked?" she asks. She looks me up and down. It seems she wonders if I could be as stupid as she suspects.

"Of course not," I say. "I always lock it."

But the door stands ajar.

The padlock lies broken on the ground.

23

Broken

For a fleeting moment, my heart lifts. Maybe Bapak has unlocked the door—he has come home. But sense tells me that isn't what has happened. Why would Bapak break the lock?

My stomach flip-flops, and my heart pounds hard in my chest. I am still shaky from the mob attack. Ibu Jaga pushes me forward. My legs wobble but I nudge the door open.

The shack is empty. Whoever was here is gone. Ibu Jaga follows me inside, making *tsk-tsk* sounds and shaking her head as we look around. It is as though a storm has blown through it. The kettle lies in the middle of the floor, its lid missing. I know before I look inside that it will be empty. And it is. All the money is gone.

Our pots and pans and cooking utensils are scattered around the room. Flour and sugar is tipped onto the floor. Dirt from muddy shoes has been ground into the ingredients, making it impossible to save. The woven mat is partly rolled up on the floor. My spiral notebooks with all my stories in them are scattered everywhere. The mattress has been moved, and the bedcover is screwed up into a ball. Our clothes have been flung about and lie in odd-looking shapes around the room. Whoever has been here has upturned every item in the room.

Mama's chest is still in its place in the corner, but the lid gapes open like the mouth of a dead animal. I can barely stand to peer inside. I feel sick to my stomach. All the contents—Mama's wedding garments and golden comb—are gone.

I crouch on the floor and cover my face with my hands. I can't even cry anymore. What will happen to me and Rudi? Bapak is gone. I have no money. No money to pay rent. No money to buy food or supplies for making the fritters. I stay on the floor. I pray to Mama to help me. I pray for her to tell me what to do.

"Do you know who did this?" Ibu Jaga stands over me, her arms crossed over her chest.

I shake my head.

"You need to think harder."

"How? How can I know who did this?" I look up at her.

"Think harder," she says again, and taps her forehead. I study Ibu Jaga's face. What does she know? What is she not telling me?

Yuli bursts through the door. "Nia!" she cries, rushing to me. "I heard about the market. Are you okay? Are you hurt?" Yuli stops in her tracks. She looks around the room. "What a mess!"

I throw my arms around Yuli and hold on tight.

"I've missed you so much," I tell her. "I'm sorry."

Yuli nods and kisses my cheek. "Me too." She draws away, still holding my hands. "What happened here?" she asks.

"I was robbed."

"Everything?" she asks.

I nod.

"Oh, Nia."

Yuli notices Ibu Jaga and her eyebrows crease in confusion.

"Ibu Jaga saved me," I say. "If it weren't for her, I would be charcoal by now."

"Stop. Don't say such things," says Yuli as she sits down next to me.

"It's true," I say. "You weren't there."

"I'm so glad you're okay." Yuli puts her arms around me and I sink into them.

Ibu Jaga claps her hands together loudly. "No time for this. More important things to do." Ibu Jaga fixes me with her hard gaze. "Think harder," she says. "Who has stolen from you? Who did this?"

Yuli releases me from her embrace, still holding my hand. "Yes, think," she says. "Who would steal from you?"

My mind scans over the horrible day. Many people are angry with me. Many people might have cause to rob me. The martabak seller's face flashes in my mind. Does he know where I live?

"Who has unfinished business with you?" Ibu Jaga urges.

Then it comes to me in a flash.

"Oskar," I say. "He said he knew where I lived and that he had unfinished business with Bapak. Who else would take mama's wedding garments but a tailor?"

I look from Yuli to Ibu Jaga. "Oskar said he had business with Bapak. He seemed mad when I told him my father was away. Maybe he took the money and Mama's things to get back at Bapak," I say. "I have to find out."

"But how?" asks Yuli. "Your bapak isn't here to help you."

Going to the police is not a consideration. Police are not interested in catching a poor person who steals from a poorer person.

The only one I can think of to help me is Jango. He knows everyone. Maybe Bapak had told him what he was up to with Oskar.

Ten minutes later I am pounding on Jango's door again. "Jango!" I shout. He finally opens the door.

"You have to help me," I tell him.

24

One-Eyed Dog

I grip the minibus's handrail and close my eyes. But that makes it worse. All I can think of is the last time I took a minibus. I open my eyes and focus on the traffic outside the window instead. An endless stream of motorbikes, scooters, and cars hoot their horns and jockey for space on the road. The bus is full and we are squeezed between pointy elbows. I am jostled with every jolt of the minibus as it makes its way through the congested city traffic. I watch a woman walking on the edge of the road, balancing an orange bucket full of water on her head. She holds a cloth to her face to block the stench of car fumes.

"Here," says Jango, who is sitting next to me. "Come on."

We push our way out of the minibus and step onto the side of the road. I breathe a sigh of relief to be free of the bus.

"Come on," he says, rushing ahead. "This way. Keep up."

After some pleading, Jango agreed to help me find Oskar's shop. He stayed tight-lipped about Bapak. If he knows of any unfinished business with Oskar, he isn't saying so. But he finally agreed to help me. Maybe because of Mama, or maybe to shut me up.

We enter Pasar Senen and I'm reminded of the day of the accident when Oskar led me through the same stalls, although nothing looks familiar. Jango stops in front of a small shop. It is closed with a security gate pulled over the door and window. A gold-lettered sign on the door says: MAGNIFICENT VIP TAILOR!

"Is this it?" Jango points at the small storefront.

"That sounds like him all right," I say, reading the sign. "But the shop is much smaller than I imagined. There's no one inside." I peer between the bars of the security gate and through the window.

"No, but we can take a look and see what he has," says Jango.

"We can't break in. What if we get caught?"

"Isn't this what you wanted? Your mama's things might be in there."

He squats in front of the store and takes the backpack

off his shoulder. He reaches inside and pulls out a large metal tool.

"It's called a crowbar," he says, before I can ask. He motions to the door. "Do you want in or not?"

I pace in front of the store. "But what if it wasn't him?"

"You won't know until we search inside."

I look around to see if anyone is watching us. It is dusk. The street is filled with the sweet smoky fragrance of barbecued satay. Cooks from street stalls fan chicken and goat skewers over hot coals, sending up billows of smoke. Shoppers go about their business without giving us a second glance. A man in a crisp white shirt has dozens of women's purses slung over both shoulders. "Designer brands!" he calls as he makes his way down the street. A scooter speeds past with three boys riding together, still wearing their school backpacks. Only a scrawny one-eyed street dog is looking our way, and it soon limps off.

I think of Mama's wedding clothes and her golden comb. I can't imagine never seeing them again. Not to mention the money.

I nod to Jango and watch in silence as he jimmies the crowbar under the security gate. He pulls and levers it until we hear a snap. He grips the security gate and yanks upward. It rolls up fast and makes a loud bang when it hits the top. I look around to see if anyone on the street has noticed. A shrimp-cracker hawker walks past, paying us no attention. Everyone on the street is only concerned with their own business. Jango reaches for another tool in his backpack and uses it to snap open the lock.

We stand inside the small space that is Oskar's tailor shop. The shelves are stacked with fabrics: checks, stripes, batik prints, and flowery designs. In the middle of the small room sits an ancient sewing machine, and behind it stands a mannequin without a head. The mannequin wears Oskar's blue suit jacket. His purple tie hangs open around its neck.

I scan the shelves for Mama's things. I know the fabrics by heart—they are embedded in my mind.

"There!" I say, and point to a shelf. "And there!"

I grab her wedding kebaya and hold them to my chest. "It really was him," I say to Jango. "I can't believe he would do it. I always thought he was nice…maybe a bit annoying, but harmless."

Jango nods. He doesn't seem surprised.

"But her wedding comb is still missing," I say.

"And the money," says Jango as he checks every inch of the room.

We search each shelf but can't find anything.

"Take whatever you want," says Jango, gesturing to the stacks of fabrics. "We'll come back tomorrow and ask him about the money. But be quick. We need to get out of here."

"I'm not going to steal," I tell him. "I'm not going to become a thief." The accusation from the martabak seller and the angry mob still jangles in my head.

"You'll just be getting even," says Jango. "He stole from you. Your money is gone but you can take some of his stuff to make up for it."

"I will take Mama's things back but nothing else. If I did, that would make me as bad as he is."

"Suit yourself," he says, and fills his backpack with garments. "I don't have a problem with such ideas." Jango holds two shirts up to his chest. "Check or stripe?"

He looks at me and winks.

25

Surprises

I have never seen our shack so tidy since before Mama died. The mat is swept clean, and it has been returned to its place in the center of the room. The pots, pans, and utensils are stacked neatly on the shelf. Our clothes are folded and tucked away in Mama's chest. The mattress is freshly made with a clean bedspread. Harmony has been restored.

My gaze finds the kettle sitting on the kitchen shelf. Has it all been a dream? If I look inside the kettle, will the money be returned?

"You're back." Ibu Jaga stands at the front door.

I motion around the room. "Did you do this?"

"I told you I would before you left," she says matter-of-factly. "You were in too much of a hurry to listen. I cooked also." She shuffles to the kitchen shelf and pulls down a saucepan. She opens the lid and shows me a thick curry inside. It is bright yellow from turmeric powder. "Carrots, potatoes, and beans," she says, putting her nose close to the saucepan and sniffing the contents.

"Thank you," I say finally. "You have been so kind to me. I don't know how—"

Rudi bursts through the door. He rushes in ahead of Yuli. "Nia!" he yells, running into my legs. "It is already dark and you didn't come to get me."

I hold on to him tight. I feel I might cry again.

"You're squeezing the air out of me," he says finally, and I let him go.

Yuli looks at me expectantly. "So? What happened?" she urges. "Did you find anything at the tailor's?"

I am so relieved to have Yuli back. "Let's all eat," I say, sitting on the mat. "And I'll tell you what happened."

Rudi, Yuli, and I sit down. I begin to spoon Ibu Jaga's curry into bowls, and pass them around.

Ibu Jaga remains standing. "Not me," she says. "I have work to do."

"It's already nighttime," I say to her. "Please eat with us. You cleaned the entire place and cooked this food. You should eat. Please."

"I have already eaten."

"Ibu, I know that I owe you money for today…for the shower…I will repay you."

Ibu Jaga looks at me steadily. "You will repay me when the time comes." She turns and walks toward the door. She stops and grunts at it. "Keep this locked," she says, and then she's gone.

Yuli raises her eyebrows. "That was weird," she says as she spoons curry into her mouth. "I thought she hated you."

"Me too," I say. "But if it weren't for her, I don't know what would have happened today. I think I owe her my life."

I eat the curry and tell Yuli what Jango and I found at Oskar's tailor shop.

Rudi is intent on his bowl. "Why haven't you cooked this before?" he asks. "It's so good. Can I have more?"

"I can't believe it," says Yuli. "The thief."

"Believe it," I say, getting up to hook the inside latch on the door as Ibu Jaga said to do. "I have the proof."

Before I close the door, I look out into the alley. I can barely believe my eyes when I see who is walking briskly toward me.

"My sweet girl," Oskar says as he arrives at the door. "What a relief to see that you are all right. I heard what happened at the market. What a terrible business. Terrible." He looks me up and down. "You appear to be in one piece, thank God."

I am speechless. Then anger rises up in me like a tidal wave.

"You!" I yell. "How dare you come here? I know what you did. I know it was you."

I go inside to get Mama's wedding garments. "Here," I say, thrusting them in front of his face. "I found these at your shop. You stole from me. Where is my money? Where is Mama's comb?"

Oskar looks bemused. "Oh, that was you at my store? I see."

"This is not funny!" I say to him. "Give me the money and the comb. Give me what belongs to me."

Yuli has come to stand beside me. "Do as she says, *thief*."

"My girl, I assure you I am not a thief. I am well within my rights."

"What are you talking about? What rights? You broke in here and stole from me."

"No," he says. "I was merely ensuring I would receive what I have been promised."

"Promised?" I shriek. "Promised by *who*?"

Oskar looks from me to Yuli and back again. "Your father, of course." He tilts his head slightly. "He didn't tell you? I was promised a dowry."

He places his hands on his chest and smiles. "My dearest Nia, we are to be married."

26

A Girl Like You

The force of Oskar's declaration almost knocks me off my feet. I stagger into the house and sit on the mat. Yuli keeps guard at the door, blocking Oskar's entry.

"May I come in to explain?" asks Oskar.

I motion for Yuli to let him inside. Oskar enters reluctantly and looks around as if he might become contaminated.

"Sit," says Yuli, motioning to the mat. I watch in silence as Oskar glances at the mat uncomfortably. "Don't worry, you won't catch anything," says Yuli dryly. "Believe it or not, we know how to keep things clean, even here in the slum."

"Thank you, but I will stand," says Oskar.

"Who is this?" Rudi asks. He is still sitting on the mat next to me. He has helped himself to a second bowl of curry.

"I will be your older brother one day," says Oskar. "You can call me Mr. Oskar for now."

"No you will not," I say. "Rudi, don't listen to him." I look up at Oskar. "I don't care what my father promised you. I am not going to marry you. I am not going to marry anyone. Not for a long time. I am going to high school. Then after that, I am going to earn a scholarship to become a writer. I have a future away from here. I—"

"Yes, you do," he says, interrupting me. "That much is true. My mother's house is not so far from here, and that is where we will live." He looks at me as if I were a small child. "I am sorry this news comes to you as a shock. But if you give yourself time to think it over, you will realize this is news worthy of celebration." He shifts from foot to foot. "You will live in a real house with electricity and running water!" He flings his arms around. "I can give you a decent life. More than a girl like you could hope for. You won't need to bother yourself with school." He thinks for a moment. "But I guess we could find some books for you to read if you like that kind of thing."

As a train thunders by, the walls shake. "I would think you would be more grateful," Oskar adds, once the train has passed. "It took some time to convince my mother, but I assured her you are an excellent cook and that you will bring us good luck. You see," he went on, "aside from your beauty, I truly do believe you are blessed with good-luck magic. And you need not be worried. I know you are very young. We will wait until you are sixteen at least. But since your father has left, you might as well come and live in my mother's house now. She needs some help to cook and clean." He sighs. "She continues to have a lot of trouble finding a helper to do the work to her liking."

"No," I say simply. "I won't."

"My dear, I am sorry to say that you do not have a choice. Your father promised."

"He will un-promise."

"Where is he?" says Oskar, waving his arms around the space. "I do not see him anywhere. He has left you un-protected. Look what happened to you at the market. You have no money. You are lucky I am here to help you. I will even make a space for your brother."

"I will find my father," I say assertively. "I will find him, and he will break his promise to you. I will not be your wife. I will not be your mother's servant."

"You are being very foolish," says Oskar, studying me and shaking his head. "But I suppose I can understand that you would be muddled in the head after such a trau-matic experience today." He sighs and looks around the room. "I will return tomorrow once you've had a chance to think things over." He goes to the door. Then he turns once more before leaving. "And under the circumstances,

I forgive you for breaking into my shop."

"Well, I don't forgive you for trashing my house and stealing my money and my mother's things."

"It is true my mother got carried away in her search for the dowry. My apologies." He clears his throat. "She was in quite a fury."

"It was your mother who made that mess?"

"I am sorry. She will ask your forgiveness once we are family, I am sure." Although judging by his sheepish expression, he looks anything but sure. "Here," he says, taking some rupiah from his wallet. "Here is some money for now." I don't want to take it but Yuli elbows me. It's probably the money he has taken from me anyway.

I sit in silence as Oskar finally leaves. I put my head in my hands and feel Yuli's hand on my back.

"Can this day get any worse?" I ask her after a while. "Please tell me it can't."

Yuli squeezes my shoulder. "Maybe you should think about marrying him."

I sit bolt upright again. "What? No! I am not going to think about it. Why would I think about it?"

"He isn't so bad. He's young. He is sweet in a way. He has his own business, and he wears nice clothes. Shouldn't you at least visit the house and take a look?"

"No! I don't care about his mother's house. I am not going to marry Oskar. You marry him if you think he isn't so bad."

"He doesn't want me. He wants you and your good luck."

"Would you actually think about it, if he did ask you?"

She lifts a shoulder. "Maybe."

"Not me. I have to find Bapak. He needs to fix this."

Yuli takes a deep breath. "I have something to tell you. It's...well, it's not exactly bad...considering."

I look up at her. "What is it?"

"Your bapak," she says. "He isn't in Lembang. I know where he is. Jango told me."

"What? Where is he?"

"He's living with a woman and her baby in a shanty-town near Cikini Station." Yuli pauses and reaches for my hand. "People say that the baby is his."

My head rattles as I try to make sense of the information. I think of all the nights he didn't come home after drinking at Jango's. All those nights when he left Rudi and me alone.

"Why didn't you tell me sooner?"

Yuli twists her lips nervously. "Because I knew you would be upset. Besides, it's not like we have been talking lately."

It is true. The last thing I want to do is argue with her now we're friends again.

"But you see," says Yuli, trying her best to sound cheerful. "It was best that I waited after all, wasn't it? Because now it's not such bad news."

27

Dreams to Remember

Mama nudges me awake. "Baby, wake up," she whispers in my ear. "It's your time now."

I open my eyes and look around me. It is dark. Mama is sitting on the edge of the mattress and smiling down at me. A luminous light glows all around her.

"You will look so pretty in my kebaya one day," she says, tracing my face with her fingertips. "My girl is a young woman now."

"Mama," I say, and I reach for her. "Please help me. Something terrible has happened. I am all alone. I need help. Please, Mama. Please help me. Please tell me what to do."

Mama ignores my distress. She flaps her hand at me like she used to when I would complain about sweeping the floor or helping her fetch water.

"It's time for you to wear my kebaya." She looks pleased and not upset at all. "You will look so beautiful," she adds.

Mama has her wedding kebaya in her hands.

"Here," she says, holding up the lace blouse—a rich emerald green. Then she holds up the matching batik sarong with its intricate floral design in golds, greens, and pinks. "Wrap the sarong around your waist." Mama's face is bright with excitement.

I lay still and gaze into her beautiful face. I feel the tears stream down my cheeks. "It doesn't matter. I can't do it anymore," I tell her. "I'm too tired. I have failed at everything. I have lied to people about being magic. I lost all our money, and Bapak is gone. I have done everything wrong."

"Shhhh...," she says. "You are tired, that's all. Sleep now. I will stay here and watch you, I promise."

I feel Mama's touch on my eyelids, gently closing them. "Shhhh...," she says again. "I'll tell you a story and you will fall back to sleep."

When I wake up she is gone. I am still lying on the mattress, and I am clutching her kebaya, the garments

Jango and I had gone to so much trouble to retrieve. I fell asleep holding them.

Later that morning, I am sitting in the cab of a charcoal delivery truck. The truck driver is a friend of Jango's who has agreed to take me to the shantytown in Cikini, where Bapak is living. It has been no secret apparently—to everyone except me—where he lives and with whom. The driver doesn't speak to me much. He chain-smokes clove cigarettes and squints at the traffic through the dirty windshield. Cikini is not far from Senen, but with the traffic and the driver's deliveries, it takes over an hour.

I watch the street hawkers dodge in and out of stopped traffic, trying to sell their wares. They are mostly young boys like Jojo with trays of tobacco, candies, and bottled water. Some tap on closed windows, holding their goods up to the glass.

I told Yuli that I would never marry Oskar, but what if Bapak won't help me? What if he won't set things right? What choice do I have then? Girls are arranged in marriage all the time. It is the old way. We are meant to do as we are told. We are not meant to have our own dreams. Who am I to turn down a chance to have a real roof over our heads? Is it selfish of me to want to go to school instead?

I try to prepare myself to see Bapak again. I look at myself in the mirror. It is Mama's worried face that looks back at me.

Be strong, she tells me in the mirror.

A familiar sight lies in front of me. Bapak is splayed out on a dirty mat in a tiny fall-down shack of a room. He is asleep and snoring. The smells of sweat, alcohol, and vomit waft around the small, hot space. A young woman sits in the corner of the room. She cradles a sleeping infant in her arms. The tiny, sweating baby is wrapped in a filthy sarong. Flies circle the child's face, and the woman swats them away as best she can.

"I have to speak to him." I point to the heap on the floor. "I am his daughter."

The woman just nods. She is young—maybe eighteen or nineteen. She keeps her eyes downcast and clings to the child. I have no quarrel with this woman and her baby.

I stand above Bapak, my hands on my hips. I nudge him with my foot.

"Wake up," I say loudly.

He rolls and groans. I continue to prod him harder until he finally opens his eyes. He holds his elbow in front of his face to block the light.

"Wake up," I say again. "Get up."

Wide-eyed, Bapak stares at me. "Nia," he mutters. He rubs his eyes. "I don't understand. How—how?"

"Get up," I repeat. "You are a disgrace. Get up and do as I say."

Bapak sits up, looking confused. I hand him a bottle of water. He guzzles half of it before I snatch it away from him. I hand it to the woman and she nods in thanks.

"You have to come with me," I say to him. "Now."

Bapak continues to sit and stare at me with a puzzled expression. He rubs his eyes again, his mouth agape. "Nia," he says again.

I grab a hold of his t-shirt and yank him upward. "Come on. Up. Get up. You have to come with me." He staggers to his feet and sways before righting himself.

"Nia." he focuses on me, at a loss. "It's you. I—I—"

"Save your words," I say. "We will have plenty of time to talk on our way back home. You have a lot to answer for." I push him toward the door. He is dazed, still drunk and half-asleep, but he allows me to herd him out.

The girl bows her head. "Please," she says. "We are hungry. He promised he would marry me and that he would take care of us. But all he does is drink arak and spend the money I earn mending clothes. We have barely enough to buy rice."

"He is good at making false promises," I say. I give her the few rupiah I have in my pocket. "I have no more to give."

I look around the stuffy room. I know what this feels like.

"I will make sure he does not abandon you and your baby. You will not be left alone, I promise you."

28

Not Your Promise To Give

We travel back in the delivery truck. Bapak sits in the flatbed with the bags while I ride in the cab.

"I did go back to the village in Lembang," Bapak says, once we are back at home and he has cleaned up. "I went to see if I could sell my land to my brothers." He looks up and meets my eyes. "I wanted to get money for…for all my children." He looks around. "Where is Rudi?"

I want to shout, *What do you care? You have never cared about Rudi. I am the one who has raised him and loved him.* But I know if I am to get through this and have Bapak do as I wish, I have to be careful with my words.

"He is at school."

Bapak nods. "Of course."

"What happened, Bapak?" I ask him. "With your brothers?"

"They would not sell to me," he says in a sulky tone. "They would not even give me the money they had received for renting my land to grow rice."

"Why not?"

"My brothers said they did not trust me. One of the old women in the village said I had a demon inside me." He pauses. "Maybe it is true."

"There is no demon. No one is to blame except you," I say coldly. "But your brothers are right. You have not honored your duties to us. You have chosen arak instead."

Bapak hangs his head, then raises it again. He implores me with his eyes. "My family would not give me money. What could I do?"

"Do you know what you have done? What has been happening here? You lied to Rudi. You left me to take care of everything." My hands are balled into fists. "And you promised me in marriage to Oskar."

Bapak nods. "Yes, I did. It is a good opportunity for you."

"A good opportunity for *you*, you mean. How could you do that without asking me? How could you give me away without even thinking about what I want?" My voice is rising to a hysterical pitch. *I must calm down*, I tell myself. *I must make him understand*. "Haven't I always been a good daughter? Haven't I always taken care of Rudi and done everything that Mama would have done?"

"He is a kind man, a good man. He has prospects. He can give you a better life. I was only thinking about your future."

"I don't want a life with Oskar. I want my own life. I want to go to school. You know this. I have dreams. I want to become a writer one day."

"We all want things, Nia," I can see Bapak's temper rising. "But it's not possible. We have no money. Oskar's offer makes good sense. He will take care of you—and Rudi as well. You will never be hungry and you will be protected."

"We will be his mother's servants. That's what will happen to us. And you will be rid of your responsibility to us. That's what you really want, isn't it? To be rid of us."

Bapak scowls. His face has turned red. "You are an ungrateful daughter."

"No. You are a selfish father." I can't stop my anger. "We have no money because you waste it all on arak. Do you know that a mob almost set me on fire at the market yesterday?" I see his eyes widen in shock, but I can't stop myself. I want to hurt him. "You were not here to protect us. You call yourself a father, but you are nothing more than a drunk. You are a disgrace. Mama would be ashamed of you. She would never forgive you for how you treated us. You have dishonored her memory by taking up with that girl."

His slap is sharp, and the pain flashes bright. The blow almost knocks me off balance.

I put my hand against my face to stop the stinging. Tears immediately spill down my cheeks.

I can see the instant regret on his face. We lock eyes.

He hunches over and begins to sob. "Nia, I am sorry. Please, forgive me. I have lost my way. I am sorry. I am sorry. Please forgive me."

He keeps sobbing and begging for forgiveness. But I am unmoved.

"I was a better man once," he moans. "For her. I was a better man for your mama. But I will never be that man again. Never again, not without her."

"Yes you will," I begin quietly. "You can still do your duty and take care of your children. You can still honor her memory." I take a deep breath. "You can still choose the right way."

He holds his head in his hands and slowly nods.

"We will go together to Oskar's home," I say firmly, "and we will get back Mama's wedding comb and the money he took for my dowry. You *will* do this or I'll never forgive you. Mama will never forgive you.

"And you will break your promise to Oskar. I am not your promise to give."

29

A Girl Like Me?

After I drop Rudi off at school the next morning, I return home to prepare for our visit to Oskar's. I study Mama's clothes folded on the chest in the corner. I think of my dream of Mama. I remember the hundreds of times I have taken her clothes out of that chest and imagined wearing them.

"You are right, Mama," I say. "Today is the day to wear your kebaya."

I slip the emerald green blouse around my shoulders and fasten the buttons. Then I wrap the batik sarong and tie it tightly around my waist like I had seen Mama do many times. I smooth the fabric against my skin and brush out my long hair. I feel transformed somehow. The only item missing is her golden comb.

Bapak arrives shortly afterward. "Come," he says. "Jango gave me the address." If Bapak is surprised to see me dressed in Mama's kebaya, he doesn't say anything. I guess he's tired of arguing with me.

Bapak and I travel the distance to Oskar's house by rickshaw. Oskar's neighborhood isn't far from Pasar Senen, where his tailor shop is located. It is not a wealthy area but it's far from slum living. The modest houses are painted white—some with palms planted in the small front yards.

"Are you sure this is it?" I ask him when the rickshaw pulls up.

Bapak nods. "Yes, this is it. He is expecting us, I called ahead."

We climb out of the rickshaw and Bapak gives the driver the coins. Oskar's house, like many others, has a security gate that runs across the width of the property. It's over two yards high, with barbed wire on top.

I press the buzzer on the outside of the gate. I keep my finger on the button until a houseboy shuffles down the drive. He opens a small peephole in the gate and looks at us suspiciously.

"Why all the noise? Who are you?"

"My name is Nia, and this is my father. We are here to see Oskar."

The houseboy continues to look at us warily, as if he can't decide what to do.

"It's fine, it's fine." I hear Oskar's voice behind the houseboy. "Open the gate."

I hear the heavy latch being pulled aside, and the gate slowly rolls open.

"Come in." Oskar holds his arm up to usher us inside. "I am very glad you are here," he adds. "I am pleased to see you have changed your mind. Come in, come in."

I stop in my tracks as I hear the gate lock behind me.

"No—," I start to say, but Bapak grips my arm tightly to hush me.

Oskar and Bapak exchange a look.

"Please come inside," says Oskar. "Let us talk properly. My mother is waiting."

Bapak pushes me forward and speaks in my ear. "Calm down, Nia. We do not want him to lose face. Let me speak first."

My stomach churns. Is this a trick? Can I trust Bapak to do as he promises?

Oskar leads us through the front door into a receiving room with four brown leather sidechairs and a low table with a leafy green plant sitting on it.

"Please sit down," he says, motioning to the chairs. "My mother will join us shortly."

I sit and look around the room. The floor is laid with sparkling white tile, and family portraits hang on the walls.

I recognize Oskar in many of them. The air conditioning makes me shiver. Through a doorway leading to the rest of the house, I catch sight of a young woman on her hands and knees cleaning the floor tiles with a blue towel.

An older woman walks slowly into the room. I recognize her from the photos as Oskar's mother. She is wearing a housedress and slippers. She is not smiling. Her hair is lacquered up in the old style. I wonder absently if Big Sula's mama did it for her.

Oskar's mother turns and gestures angrily to the young woman cleaning the floor, and the maid scurries off.

"Mother, please come and meet Nia and her father."

Bapak and I bow our heads slightly and put our palms together in the traditional Javanese greeting. She acknowledges our gesture and perches on a chair as far away from us as possible. Her expression is almost a sneer. I wonder if she is concerned about the state of her leather chairs with us sitting on them.

The maid who was cleaning the floor arrives with a tray of tea-filled glasses. The glasses clink as she sets the tray down hesitantly on the table. She keeps her eyes downcast and shuffles backward from the room.

"You look very beautiful today, Nia," says Oskar.

He thinks I dressed this way for him, I realize. I turn to Bapak and stare at him pointedly. Bapak coughs and looks away.

Oskar smiles hopefully and moves the tea glasses toward us across the table. "Please, please, let's drink some tea and talk."

"Thank you for having us in your home," says Bapak finally. "I...I...my daughter...well, you see, she—" He seems incapable of finding the words.

"What he is trying to say," I burst out, "is that I do not wish to marry Oskar, and so my father must break his promise to you."

Oskar appears stricken.

"My apologies," says Bapak. "My daughter, she is headstrong...she is like her mother."

His mother shakes her head, making *tsk-tsk* noises. "I told you this was a bad idea," she says to Oskar. "Why would we get mixed up with their kind? They do not even know the value of a promise."

Oskar bows his head like a chastised child.

"Good riddance to garbage," she says, swatting the air. "How dare you come here and insult my son? Go! Be gone with you."

"We will go once you return our money and my mother's gold comb," I say.

"The insolence! To think we offered a girl like you a place in our home, and now you dare to throw it back in our faces. We owe you nothing."

"A *girl like me*?" I ask her.

I am suddenly sick and tired of hearing this. I've had a lifetime of being addressed this way. Sneered and scoffed at like Oskar's mother is doing, looking down her nose at me. Today it will end.

I shoot up from my seat. I sweep my arms out and around me, as if I were gathering waves.

"You don't know who I am," I say boldly. "You have misjudged me. You just see a poor girl, but that is not who I am."

Oskar's mother scoffs at me but I continue to hold her gaze.

My voice is steady and strong. "I am the Girl of the Southern Sea. I hold all the power of the ocean. I own the riches of the deep, and I will live forever. I can defeat sea serpents and I can conjure tidal waves. I am not afraid of you."

All three stare at me as if I have suddenly gone mad. And maybe I *have* gone a little mad. But in this moment, I am Dewi Kadita. I am the Girl of the Southern Sea.

"All you see is a poor girl," I go on. "A girl without power or choices. But you are wrong. I am here to live a different story. I am here to write my own story."

I continue to gather imaginary waves around me.

"Give me what belongs to us," I demand.

Oskar looks afraid. He has always believed that I was magic. He glances at his mother, who tilts her head slightly. Oskar gets up and leaves the room. I stand my ground as I glare at his mother. She returns my gaze defiantly, but I also catch an expression of hesitation and uncertainty. I do not break eye contact with her.

Oskar comes back with a plastic bag that he hands to me.

"We were only holding this for your safekeeping, you understand," he says. "We did not mean any harm."

I look in the bag. Mama's comb and a roll of rupiah are inside.

"You will not bother me or my family again," I tell him.

Then I stride out the door, not bothering to see if Bapak is behind me or not.

30

A Mother's Tears

Mama visits me again.

I see her from a distance bent down by the side of the river. It is the same river where she had washed my hair before. Except this time it is not night. There is no blanket of star-jewels. Now it is dawn, and the sky is illuminated by a golden glow. The trees and water reflect the early sun's warm amber light. It looks as if Mama is washing clothes in the river, but she has her back to me.

"I will help you, Mama," I call to her. But she doesn't turn around. It feels as if it takes a long time for me to reach her by the river's edge. "Mama," I call

again. "I will help you. Please wait!"

I finally get close enough to touch her shoulder. "Mama," I say. "Here I am."

She turns around, and I see streams of tears running down her face. Now that I am closer, it seems as though the river is made of the tears that have spilled from her eyes.

"Don't worry," she says. "A mother's tears flow straight to Heaven." Then she points upriver. "And all rivers lead to the ocean."

She stands up and shows me what she holds in her hands—this is what she has been cleaning in the river. It's her golden comb. "You returned it to me," she says. "I am so proud of you, my daughter." She strokes my cheek and hands the comb to me. "It is yours now. You will wear this on the most important day of your life." She smiles. "It is time. It is dawn."

She looks toward the golden, rising sun. Her tears have dried now.

"No, Mama. Stay with me," I plead. "Please don't go yet."

"Nia, my beautiful princess," she says. "I have never left you." She bends down to kiss the golden comb in my hands, and presses it to my heart.

"I am always here."

I promise Yuli I'll go with her to the Internet café at the train station. She wants to send an email to a Canadian tourist she has befriended. Her latest goal is to become a model, ever since he told her he would put photos of her on his travel blog. I am relieved, because her new ambition means she has stopped working for Jango.

On the way, we stop in to see Tomi, my baby half brother, and his mother, Suna. A few weeks have passed since I brought Bapak home. He has moved Suna and Tomi to a shack along the train tracks, close enough for him to set up the cart at the Senen Station market. He is still selling fried bananas, and Suna has begun to cook and sell *lumpia* as well. Suna's spring rolls are very good.

I still wake early to make the banana batter because I make it the best. The fried-banana chant has never left my head. Besides, the cart still has my name on the front.

"Hello," I say to Suna, poking my head in the door.

"Hello, Nia." Suna beckons us inside.

I hand Suna a bag with some of Rudi's old baby clothes in it. Tomi is asleep on the single mattress. I stroke his plump cheeks and he smiles in his sleep.

"He looks well," I say.

Suna nods. "He is well."

"Bapak is at the market?" I ask, and she nods.

"I will join him once Tomi wakes up," she says. "Mama Tutti told me she will help with Tomi while I cook the lumpia."

Mama Tutti is happy to have a new baby to dote on. She is a part of our complicated family after all. She told me the other day that she caught sight of Oskar in the market, and she chased after him with her pineapple slicer. "His skinny little behind was too fast for me."

I don't know if this story is true, but I know it's Mama Tutti's way of telling me she is sorry for her part in the magic fried-bananas scam. I also know that Oskar is too much of a coward to approach me again. Besides, he has nothing to gain from me anymore.

But other faces still haunt me. Sometimes I catch glimpses of men at the market, and I wonder if they had been in the mob that day.

"No one will admit to playing a part in that crowd," Mama Tutti says when I asked her about it. "People become faceless in a mob—that's what attracts and protects them. I've seen many mob attacks in my time. That martabak seller will not show his face around this market again—this much I know for sure."

I look around Suna's room before I leave. It is a single room with no water or electricity. There is only one mattress to sleep on and one woven mat to sit on. But Tomi no longer looks so skinny and Bapak is working at the market every day. Jango says that he is keeping his nose clean. For the time being anyway. This is just as well, considering he has two households to support.

Still, each day holds the potential for everything to fall apart again.

We all balance on a knife's edge.

31

My Promise

It is predawn and I can hear the first call to prayer from the local mosque when Ibu Jaga arrives at the door. I light the kerosene lamp and unlock the latch to let her in. She shuffles inside without a smile or greeting. She holds out a plastic bag.

"Here," she says. "Sit down and get to work."

I take the bag and look inside. It is full of flower stems and pandan leaves. It is for Nyadran, I realize, the Javanese tradition of making offerings at the graves before the holy month of Ramadan. "No," I say, handing the bag back to her. "I don't do that anymore, I—"

Her expression stops me mid-sentence.

"It is time," she says simply. "It is dawn."

It is dawn. I open my mouth to speak, to ask how she knows what Mama said to me in my dream. But I can guess she won't tell me.

She continues to hold out the bag to me. "I said that the time would come for you to repay me."

I take the bag again and do as I'm told. I get my basket and sit down with Ibu Jaga as she begins to pluck the petals with her gnarled fingers. With memories of Mama's delicate hands dancing over the flowers, I pick up a stem and break open the petals.

Honor our ancestors. Rose petals for love, jasmine for purity, pandan leaves for sweetness, ylang-ylang flowers for happiness, and frangipani for the eternal soul.

Mama's words fill my mind as soon as my fingers hold the delicate petals. It is as if the blessing itself were interwoven with the stems.

Once my basket is full of petals, I add an extra frangipani flower to ask for Alit's forgiveness and then another to honor Mama. I hold out the basket to show Ibu Jaga. She gives a curt nod of approval before getting up to leave.

"You will place the flowers at the cemetery," she says as she shuffles to the door. "Just as your mama used to do."

As I watch her leave, I understand the only repayment she has ever wanted was to see my offerings at the riverside cemetery. Everyone has a duty to honor the past and hope for the future. The time has come for me to do my part.

Ibu Jaga isn't just the caretaker of the dead, I realize. She is the caretaker of the living as well.

The rains have finally arrived. Later that morning, as I walk Rudi to school, we try to keep our feet out of the muddy rivulet that snakes along the alleyways.

The river has swelled with the rains. Kids dive in from the muddy riverbank, their heads popping up like corks from under the brown water.

When we reach the school gates, Rudi pulls his hand from mine.

"See you after school," I call. I watch him pushing his way through the other children to stand next to Jojo in the lineup. Before I turn to leave, I hear my name called.

"Nia!" Mr. Surat waves to me from the school entrance. "Wait, wait! I have something important for you."

I walk to meet Mr. Surat, who is holding something in his outstretched hand.

"Look what has arrived. It is a letter from the education board. It is about you."

"About me? Why?"

Mr. Surat is beaming. "Yes, you." he nods enthusiastically and shows me the letter. "I sent them your stories along with your examination scores." He points to the typed print in the letter. "I have been given permission to hire a literacy tutor for the remainder of the school year."

I don't understand what he is saying. I search his face for further explanation.

"You, Nia!" he exclaims. "I asked them if I could hire you as the literacy tutor. You have such a good way with the children."

"Me?" I can't help but hang my head in sudden disappointment. My dream of attending high school is dashed again. I hoped beyond hope that Mr. Surat was giving me news of a scholarship. "What is a literacy tutor?"

"You will help the children who struggle with learning to read." He pauses. "I know you want to attend high school, but this is a way for you to earn the funds. The wages are low, but if you work as a literacy tutor for the rest of the year, you'll earn enough for your high-school fees. You can enroll for next year. Not only that, but while working here, you will have plenty of time and the resources to write your stories."

"Does Ibu Merah know?"

"Don't mind her," he says. "There will always be people like Ibu Merah trying to block your path. But you have never let anyone keep you down, Nia, I'm pleased to see."

My mind weighs what Mr. Surat is saying. My heart lifts. It *is* good news. I can earn my own money, I can write my stories, and I can eventually go to school.

I raise my head and smile. "Thank you," I say, feeling the tears spring. "Thank you so much."

He presses the letter into my hands. "You deserve it, Nia. The education board was very impressed with your grades and your writing skills. You have earned this."

I clutch the letter, barely able to read the words myself because the tears have blurred my vision.

I know now that I will graduate one day. And on that day, I will wear Mama's golden comb. I will keep my promise to her.

I will write my own story.

32

Girl of the Southern Sea

Yuli's Canadian blogger friend emails to ask if she knows of a seaside town in West Java called Pelabuhan Ratu. He wants to know if she is willing to take the bus there from Jakarta to shoot some video on her cell phone. He'd like to know if it's a place he should recommend on his travel blog. He will send her the small amount to cover the bus fare, plus a little extra.

Yuli arrives at our shack, her eyes shining. "You and I are going to Pelabuhan Ratu," she says. "We're going to eat fresh coconut and see the ocean and walk on the sand. Just like real tourists!"

I gasp. "Pelabuhan Ratu?"

It is the very place where the mythical Queen of the Southern Sea was born. Originally a fishing village, it has become a popular holiday spot. Not only that, but every year a festival is held to honor the Sea Queen.

"If we are going to Pelabuhan Ratu," I say, "we have to go on the day of the Sea Queen Festival."

Yuli's blogger friend is excited to find out about the festival and eager for photos and videos of it. Yuli and I wait the few weeks until the festival date, and at dawn we leave for the bus terminal. The ticket seller at the terminal says we have to change buses in Bogor, but the trip shouldn't take longer than four hours. We are returning in the evening so we won't have to pay for somewhere to sleep.

The bus is old and smells of sweat, but we don't care. We are on our first adventure together. The bus ride is a thrill. At first the scene out of the large bus windows is the usual bumper-to-bumper Jakarta traffic. But after an hour we enter the city outskirts and pass through nice neighborhoods with large houses set along wide, tree-lined boulevards. Yuli and I point and pretend which houses could be ours one day.

The city traffic eventually thins to a single lane as we near the mountains. Industrial areas give way to a patchwork of rice plateaus. I never knew green could have so many shades. There's the luminous light green of the young rice shoots, the emerald green of the long grasses, and the deep forest green of giant trees that overhang the roadside. The way narrows as we wind through the mountains. Yuli falls asleep and her head bumps against my shoulder as we sway around each curve.

Children along the mountain road jump and wave as we pass, just as they do at home along the Senen train tracks. Their faces remind me of my students. I have been a literacy tutor for a few weeks now. Teaching is harder than I thought—and Ibu Merah is no more welcoming than I expected—but the look on a student's face when they start to understand their letters is worth the hours of effort.

I am lucky. I am grateful.

We reach Bogor, where we will change buses. I think of Ibu Jaga and how she grew up here on a tea plantation. We can't believe how fresh and cool the air is as we step out of the bus. I wonder if Ibu Jaga experienced a different surprise when she was a girl and arrived to find Jakarta so hot.

"Breathe it in," says Yuli, swinging her arms overhead. "No pollution. Can you believe it?"

While we wait to board the next bus, we stretch our legs and Yuli buys barbecued corn. Monkeys scamper around the bus terminal and pick through the garbage.

The next bus is more crowded and we have to share our two-seat bench with another girl. She tells us she is from Bogor and that she is also going to Pelabuhan Ratu for the festival. Her uncle cooks at a seafood restaurant on the shore. She will be working as a kitchen hand for the next two days. "I can earn really good tips," she says. "When we get there, I'll show you which stall is my uncle's. He cooks the most delicious fried octopus."

Yuli and I smile at each other. We can't imagine eating anything so fancy.

After seven hours, almost double what the ticket seller told us, we finally arrive. It is well past noon.

As soon as we leave the bus, we are swept up in the bustling crowd at Pelabuhan Ratu. Yuli and I are used to crowds, but we grip each other in excitement to be here. We hold hands and allow ourselves to be shuffled along with the people toward the shore and the festivities.

I smell the salt water before I see it. Beyond the street stalls and swarms of people, I see the ocean. It is so much more beautiful than I imagined. The water is vast and the sky above it wide open. It is so blue. It is one thing to see paintings and pictures of Dewi Kadita's ocean. It is another thing completely to hear the roar of the waves and feel the salty wind on your face.

"Are you here to see the Queen of the Southern Sea?" a fruit seller calls to us. "Here," he says. "Buy her some sweet green apples. Green is her favorite color, did you know?"

Yuli stops. She sees fresh coconuts.

"I'll have two of those," she says, pointing.

The fruit seller nods his approval. "Certainly, little sister," he says, and expertly cuts away at the husks and hard shells with a machete to reveal the round nut inside. He cuts a hole and puts a straw in each coconut, and then hands them to us. "You'll know when the Queen of the Sea is here because she calms the waters and the clouds gather overhead." He winks.

Yuli pays him and we keep walking, sipping on our straws. The liquid inside is warm and sweet.

A cheer erupts as we stroll along. The road is full of people, but we can see a horse-drawn carriage slowly making its way toward us. Riding in the carriage is a woman dressed as the Queen of the Southern Sea. She wears a green kebaya and waves to the people.

Yuli is busy taking video and photos of the carriage and the pretend Queen of the Southern Sea. I leave her and walk toward the beach. The pounding surf beckons me. I walk slowly on the grainy sand toward the cascading waves. Along the shore, local fishermen have laid out offerings of rice, vegetables, flowers, and fruit to please the Sea Queen. The fishermen hope in return that she will grant good catches and fine weather.

The surf is fierce, just as I knew it would be. My Dewi Kadita does not calm the seas—she revels in the power of her ocean.

I step closer and closer to the water's edge. I am not afraid. I breathe in the ocean air and feel the salty spray on my skin. The water crashes around my feet before it is sucked away again. The pull is strong, but I stand firm against it.

I thank Dewi Kadita for her guidance and her inspiration. I thank Mama for watching over me and for instilling her courage deep within me. I feel the power that surges at my feet and builds inside me.

"I am here," I tell them both. "I am ready."

The Legend of Nyai Roro Kidul
(Dewi Kadita)

Nyai Roro Kidul is a mythological goddess from ancient Javanese mythology. She is a complex character known by many names, including Princess of the Southern Sea and Queen of the Southern Ocean.

In one of the many retellings, before she was Nyai Roro Kidul, she was Dewi Kadita, the daughter of King Munding. Her jealous stepmother had a curse put upon her and she was banished to a life in the sea where she remained eternally beautiful. There are various versions of the story that reflect the diversity of Java and its traditional folklore.

Today the legend of Nyai Roro Kidul is still prevalent in modern Indonesia. The superstition persists all over the archipelago that men must never wear green when at the beach. Often it is told that Nyai Roro Kidul will snatch men off the beach and drag them into the ocean, especially if they are handsome or are wearing green.

The beach resort of Pelabuhan Ratu and other ocean towns in West Java hold festivals in her honor each year.

Author's Note

When I was twelve years old, I traveled with my family to my father's hometown of Bandung in West Java. The train ride from Jakarta to Bandung was exciting, jammed full of people and their belongings. There was an air of celebration, because many of the commuters were returning home after working in the capital all week. The train journey in those days took three hours, wending its way through the lush mountains. Speeding over the rickety bridges and across the cavernous ravines was a heart-stopping experience. Nothing appeared to safeguard us from the two-hundred-foot drop below. My siblings and I reveled in the thrill; we held hands and peered through the dusty windows, marveling at how daring we were.

It was not the first time that I had taken this ride because we had visited my father's homeland of Indonesia many times before. But on this particular trip, when I was twelve, I became aware of what lined the train tracks in every city and village that we passed through: children, mothers, fathers, grandmothers, and grandfathers, all living their lives in whatever home they could scrape together and mend. Lean-tos made of bamboo poles with plastic roofs, corrugated iron sheds, even cardboard boxes. It was the first time I had recognized true poverty. Regardless of their living conditions, however, the children never failed to jump in excitement and wave to us as we sped by. It was as if we, the passengers, were celebrities. Their joy and happiness in glimpsing the travelers never waned.

I suppose everyone has an event in their life where the illusion of the world in which we exist is brushed aside and the truth revealed. For me, it was this train journey and the images of the shantytowns and slums that stayed with me. I found it extremely difficult to reconcile, at that age, how some could have so little and others have so much. Indeed, it is still a reality I find difficult to reconcile today.

Images of that train journey haunted me for many years. In writing this book, I am grateful to have had the opportunity to step off the train and walk among children much like those who so many years ago, and so disarmingly, helped to shape my worldview.

As an adult I lived many years throughout Indonesia. But, although this story is set in Jakarta, it is important to note that girls with lives and stories like Nia's are not confined to this region alone. Poverty; forced marriages; and lack of health care, education, and opportunities for girls are not assigned to one continent, country, culture, or religion. They are global issues that affect girls all over the world, even in developed countries.

I have chosen to donate a portion of the book's proceeds to Plan International Canada's **Because I am a Girl** initiative.

While the locations of the story are real, this story is a work of fiction. Names, characters, businesses, and incidents are a product of my imagination. Any resemblance to actual persons, living or dead, or actual events, is purely coincidental. Any faults, errors, omissions, or embellishments with regards to the setting are mine alone.

Acknowledgments

Love and thanks to Valerie Kadarusman, Rani Kadarusman, Andre Kadarusman, and Julia Kadarusman. You all walked alongside my every memory in this story. With special thanks to my brother, Andre Kadarusman, who still lives in the region and acted as my cultural sensitivity reader.

Thanks to Chandra Wohleber for her earlier and invaluable work on this project.

Thanks to Gail Winskill and Ann Featherstone for believing in this story.

And thank you to the many young women who shared their stories with me. This book is for all of you.

A portion of the proceeds from this book are being donated...

Plan International Canada is a member of a global organization dedicated to advancing children's rights and equality for girls. We are active in more than 70 countries and have been advocating for children for over 80 years.

Around the world, girls continue to face unique barriers that violate their rights and keep them from reaching their full potential. Discrimination against girls leads to grave injustices such as limited or no educational opportunities, child marriage, and gender-based violence.

Plan International Canada works with girls and young women and supports them to become leaders. Once girls are aware of their rights and have an improved social position, they can successfully advocate for change in their lives, in their community, or around the world. Plan International Canada also actively engages men and boys in our efforts to advance equality.

Get involved with Plan International Canada!

1. Start a gender equality group at your school and help drive positive change around the world

2. Join the conversation online **@PlanCanada @PlanUSA**

3. Donate to support equal rights for all children through Plan International Canada's Gifts of Hope program or through its **Because I am a Girl** initiative

4. Sponsor a child—help give the gift of a better life and build a personal connection with your sponsored child by writing letters

5. Learn more about Plan International Canada at **plancanada.ca** and about Plan International USA at **planusa.org**

Michelle Kadarusman

grew up in Melbourne, Australia, and has also lived in Indonesia on the island of Bali and in the cities of Jakarta and Surabaya on Java. Her previous novels include *The Theory of Hummingbirds* and *Music for Tigers*, which was an honor book for the Green Earth Book Award, among others. Today Michelle lives in Toronto, Canada, and Byron Bay, Australia. Her first picture book, *Room for More*, will be published in Spring 2022, and her next novel for middle-grade readers will be *Berani*, which will be published in Fall 2022.